# COUNCIL OF SHADOWS

## CLINT WESTGARD

# ALSO BY CLINT WESTGARD

*The Shadow Men:*

    *Realm of Shadows*

    *Council of Shadows*

    *Dance of Shadows*

*The Sojourners Cycle:*

    *The Forgotten*

    *The Apostate*

    *The Acolyte (forthcoming)*

    *The Double (forthcoming)*

    *The Sojourner (forthcoming)*

*The Trials of the Minotaur*

*The Maleficio Chronicles*

Published by Lost Quarter Books
www.lostquarterbooks.com

*For my family, for all their support.*

# CONTENTS

# PRINCIPAL CHARACTERS

**Craitol:**

Lastl:

*Donier a Fieled, noble of the third rank, officer in the Gver's army*

*Keleprai a Lastl, Gver of Lastl*

*Kigarle a Nepene, noble of the first rank in Lastl*

*Liene ul Terainous a Fusel, noble of rank in Lastl*

*Ludenn a Ghuerl, noble of rank, officer in the Gver's army*

*Niriese ul Keleprai a Vellar, wife of the Gver of Lastl*


Craitol:

*Alieren, Qraulla of the Realm*

*Dalenna ul Lestulatera, mother to the Qraul*

*Elihaun, Master of Offices for the Qraul*

*Laterala, Qraul of the Realm*


Other Great Families:

*Byuvir a Kylep, Gver of Kylep*

*Duirhe a Takyl, Gver of Takyl*

*Pervelte a Pysel, Gver of Pysel*

Adepts:

*Cepedutherupt, High Adept of the Council of Adepts*

*Hieran, disciple to Adept Tehh*

*Kercubegahedd, false Adept and leader of the Kragian rebellion*

*Tehh, Adept of Lastl*

*Vyissan, a Kragian and an Adept*

## Renuih:

*Ad Eselte, emperor of Renuih*

Ad Ezern:

*Ctuellan, eunuch*

*Ibrazol id Ezern, Imperial Vazeir*

*Masiph den Ibrazol id Ezern, Jetthir of the Watch, son of Ibrazol*

Ad Reteln:

*Nyzrella (Nyzren) id Reteln, daughter of Osiphan*

*Osiphan id Reteln, nohritai in Darrhyn*

*Quesin, eunuch*

*Tequihan, castulan of the Ad Reteln household*

*Usyre id Reteln ys Luzyren, wife of Osiphan*


Nohritai:

*Erise id Illied, wife of Nustef*

*Gheyuth id Lelletl, Vazeir of the Renian Army*

*Nustef id Illied, second to Masiph on the Watch, husband of Erise*


*Achelluth, member of the Watch*

*Fush, sutler in the Renian army*

*Nazeed, one of Osiphan's conspirators*

*Phariayh, camp follower in the Renian army.*

# ONE:

# HANDS UNTOUCHED BY SQUALOR

## 1

The trepidation that had nearly overwhelmed Vyissan as he first stepped toward the gates of this magnificent city disappeared in the crush and swirl of his first moments within it. *All realms*, one of his fellow travelers had referred to it as, and Vyissan understood why as he faced its enormity. No words, no sketches could do it justice. Darrhyn, that was all, for the place was without compare. It was apparent even that first night, the gate still open and full of activity, though the lamps were lit. The streets teemed with people, the hawkers still calling their wares, no one seeming to be bothered by the heat. He stopped at the first inn he could find and went to bed immediately, not even bothering with supper, and drifted to sleep as they began to play music on the street below.

After spending a few days wandering the city to gain his bearings—a fruitless enterprise, as he quickly came to understand—he made his way to the Enir ghetto, as he had been instructed, and once there to the Geshinn House. A slow journey, marked by as many wrong turns as right. The Geshinn were an important family, with holdings across the republics and in Craitol, and here too they had a palace of a building right at the heart of the ghetto. It was a hub of activity with peoples from all corners and realms walking up and down its steps.

Vyissan had a letter of introduction, and with it he was able, without too much difficulty, to secure a meeting with the main factors for the following day. There he presented his letters and explained his predicament. He needed entry to the Imperial Palace and, if such a miracle were possible, an audience with the Emperor.

The factor, whose name was Sessitol, wetted his lips nervously. "May I inquire as to the reason you seek your audience with the Ad Eselte?"

Vyissan held his hands open and said, "I understand, of course, that this is a heavy burden to ask of anyone, let alone an honorable house like yours."

"It is a burden we embrace. Your letter," Sessitol said with a gesture, "provides enough weight to counterbalance."

Vyissan smiled his thanks. "I am grateful. You asked my business in the palace, and I am afraid I must keep that private. What I require is simply to speak to someone who has the ear of the Ad Eselte. The rest I will have to manage for myself."

Sessitol thought for a time. "I could get you an audience with someone in the Imperial Vazeir's Palace. Not the man himself, you understand, but one of his administrators. We have some business in the north of the empire, north of Kulez, near the Tribal Lands. It is governed directly by the Imperial Vazeir, and we require his permission to conduct our trade." He paused and then nodded. "Yes, I think this would work. We can get you an audience with the man who we speak to on these matters. I could give you a letter stating that you would like to join in partnership with us on some trade. You would be representing our interests there and so you will need permission to go."

He halted again and Vyissan, anticipating his concern, said, "That would be perfect. Of course, I will let them know that I deceived you as well in this."

The factor nodded gravely. "That would be just. You should have no issue with this man; he will not see what you are about."

They left it at that, with Sessitol asking him to return the next day when he, ancestors willing, would have arranged the audience. The rest of that day, Vyissan spent wandering the Enir ghetto, marveling at its size and the splendor of its sanctuaries. He stopped at a chewing house and savored an extraordinary quid. The quality of the Renian aslyn was far superior to anything in Craitol. He returned to the Geshinn House the following day and was told the audience had been arranged and would take place two days later. Sessitol gave him a letter of introduction and explained the workings and customs of the Imperial Palaces, and then they bid each other farewell in the Enir manner, with a kiss and an embrace.

As he was left to his own devices for the rest of that day and the next, and because he had no way of knowing when the opportunity might next present itself, he decided to leave the ghetto and find a brothel. Determining to spare no expense, he rented a palanquin and had the carriers take him to one of the finer brothels in the city. The girl he had the first night was so delightful that he kept her for the second. She was fascinated by his beard, touching his face constantly and laughing.

The administrator proved to be a haughty fool, angry that he had to deal with the likes of Vyissan. Having to endure hostile guards at the palace gates and again at the entrance to the Vazeir's Palace had put Vyissan in a similar frame of mind, and he had to resist the urge to respond in kind.

"Why—what was your name again?" the administrator demanded.

"Atasem den Adessel, Husem," he replied.

"Why, Atasem den Adessel, should I allow an Enir from Tuissar access to the Tribal Lands?"

"The Geshinn House was kind enough—" Vyissan began.

"They are the only reason I am even deigning to see you. I am of a mind to speak with Sessitol, I must say. This is most irregular, most irregular. Do they not understand what is going on in the north? The Luessan incursions? We cannot just allow any agents to trade in our name up there. Husem Ibrazol would have my head."

"The Geshinn House was kind enough," Vyissan tried again, "to provide me with this letter and to arrange this audience for me, but they are not aware of my reasons for seeking this audience, Husem."

Confusion and rage warred across the administrator's face. "And what reason might that be?"

"My apologies, Husem, for the deception, but I am here to see the Ad Eselte on a matter of the greatest urgency."

The administrator was left dumbfounded. "The Ad Eselte?"

Vyissan did not reply immediately. He reached into his robes and handed the administrator another letter of introduction, this one with the seal of the Qraul of Craitol on it. The administrator looked ill at the sight of it.

"As the letter states, I am an emissary of the Qraul of Craitol and I have a message for the Ad Eselte's ears only."

The administrator excused himself and Vyissan was left alone for quite some time. At one point an attendant stuck his head in the room and asked if he required anything, and Vyissan wondered if he might spare a quid. When the administrator returned, the Imperial Vazeir was with him, along with several guards.

# 2

Life felt louder on Concubine Row, Hieran mused as he passed down the street, letting the wallow of voices settle around him. The call and response of the women from the second-story windows, and their potential customers passing below, mingled with wailing of the hawkers and the general murmur that accompanied any busy city street, all coalescing to form a kind song, both familiar and unpredictable. "All the realm for sale in the Row," was the saying, true in its way.

He stopped at a stand to buy a quid of aslyn, not staying to chew with the men gathered beneath its ragged awning. His time was not his own this afternoon. While he had recovered from his last incident on the Row, Tehh had been busy. Various agents were dispatched to watch the factors, while others were set at intercepting whatever mail and goods the Currlene House passed into and out of the city. From all this the Adept managed to glean where the second factor and the nephew had been going when Hieran had been attacked and, more important, discovered there was a second meeting planned for today. According to a letter from Pysel, which someone at the Custom House had copied before resealing it and sending on, it was instrumental that both factors attend to "ensure that we are represented in those discussions which will touch upon those matters of flora for which our interest should be obvious."

A lilac figured prominently in the Lastl family crest, and so there was an obvious conclusion to draw, and Tehh, for once avoiding the arcane, drew it. Before sending him off, the Adept had said, "Mind yourself. If one of them has their heads about them they will have realized you used alkemya when they attacked you. They may have their own Adept or Thaumaturge."

In other words, do not find yourself in a similar situation as last time. The old bastard had been furious—beyond furious, really— when he had found out how much the matron of the academy expected to be paid for providing sanctuary to his Disciple. It had been paid, though likely not without some bartering, knowing the Adept. And not without the esteem in which Tehh held him falling further, which Hieran had not thought possible, to such depths that even the dead in Ulternon's Hall could not see.

It was an utter disaster, for the man was legendary for his ability to hold a grudge. He was one of the most influential Adepts on the Council; even the High Adept was careful about crossing swords with him. For twenty years he and Adept Weirn had carried on a feud, each man attempting to smear the other with accusations of false craft, or conspiring to ensure that the finest Disciples and Adepts were given positions outside of the other's realm of influence. There had been murders as well. All wood to the fire of a feud that no one could recall the prime cause of. Not that it mattered; it was about far more than that now.

He soon found himself retracing his earlier steps, passing the alley where he had been attacked, an eerie sensation overcoming him momentarily. A few streets farther on, as the crowds began to thin and the academies gave way to estates and quarters for mistresses, he found what he was looking for: a large estate, three stories, surrounded by a wall. The gate was chained shut, and as he walked by he could see the shadow cast by the man on watch.

He did not break his stride as he went by, going to the end of the street before turning and making his way down the opposite street behind the estate. There was no one on it, and, when he paused to listen, no voices reached him from any of the surrounding buildings. He approached the estate wall and pulled himself up to peer over. The grounds appeared empty, from what he could see, and several trees offered cover from the main building. Moving quickly, he scrambled up and over the wall, and then across the grounds, darting from tree to tree until he came to the shadow of the estate house, positioning himself beneath a window.

After waiting for a moment to see if he had been observed, he started to search for a way into the estate. There was a door on the far end of the building, but he rejected that outright—better to announce himself at the gate. The windows were a possibility as well, but he thought it likely that the meeting would be held on the main floor, so it seemed best to avoid it if possible. That left the tree beside him, a two-pronged thing, one of its great limbs stretching up and branching off near the building, and, in particular, near a balcony that surely led into someone's quarters.

Not wanting to risk staying exposed for a moment longer, Hieran started to climb, his heart crashing against his chest as he did. Visions of a dozen swords armed with crossbows and arrows, bolts notched, emerging from within the estate to aim at him as he clung to the tree seized his mind. At least, he thought, he would not have to listen to Tehh's admonishments any longer, though knowing his luck they would meet in the Hall, where they would be bound together again. It would be his fate, Hieran thought, to have to listen to that fool's complaints for eternity.

He had to move slowly once he came to where the trunk split into two limbs, at first because he was leery of the noise the branches and leaves might stir, and then, more terrifyingly, because the bough he was on began to dip precipitously, creaking under the strain. He inched forward as far as he dared, each groan from the branch causing his heart to race. Taking a deep—and he hoped steadying—breath, he pushed himself off the bough and dropped onto the balcony. In his panic to get off the branch he nearly missed it entirely, landing awkwardly on the railing, almost spilling off it and onto the ground below.

He pitched himself forward, letting his weight carry him off the railing and onto the balcony, very nearly swearing in the process as his knee twisted underneath him, taking all of his weight, before he remembered himself. When his breathing had steadied enough that he could no longer hear it, he went to the door and, finding it open, stepped into the chambers within. The bedchambers were to his right, the door open, and he went there immediately, after closing the balcony door, to see that it was empty. From there he went to the door that he assumed led to hallway and listened for a moment. Hearing nothing, he opened it, as quietly as he could manage, and peered down the hallway. To his right was a stairway, and he could faintly hear the sound of voices from below.

He listened for a moment, but could make nothing out clearly and so returned to the chambers, searching the cabinets and dressers within. There was a writing desk that he paid particular attention to, but there were no documents within that he could even attach a clear provenance to. It was a typical estate house in the Row—deliberately anonymous. A visit to the Hall of Records had not even managed to conclusively prove who owned the estate, which was hardly surprising. The rooms exhausted and nothing found, Hieran slipped out the door and into the hall. The voices were somewhat louder now; whoever was speaking had clearly moved onto the second floor, and Hieran moved down the stairs toward them trying to see if he could make anything out.

He was nearly halfway down the staircase when one of the voices grew louder and he heard, "I'll see to it immediately, Nes Ussul."

He froze where he was almost by instinct, his hand reaching into his robe to confirm that his dagger was still there, even as he thought about the revelation that the Gver's nephew was present again. It may have saved him, for seconds later the speaker of those words emerged from the room below, stepping out onto the staircase. The next moments passed as slowly as any in Hieran's life.

He recognized who it was immediately. His face was still marked by the alkemya burns he had received from their struggle in the alley. The man glanced up before he started down the stairs looking, it seemed to Hieran, right at where he was standing, immobile and obvious as the statue of a Qraul in a town square. Somehow, though, the man did not see him, and he turned and continued down, disappearing below.

Hieran stood rooted where he was, knowing he had to move, to hide himself, before the man or someone else came up the stairs and saw him. He tried to urge himself down, to see if he could find some vantage point where he could listen to the meeting. Here, after all, was the proof they needed Ussul and the Currlene were conspiring together. But it was not in him, not this day.

He turned and went back up the stairs, telling himself that he would search the other rooms first, give himself a moment to calm his jangled nerves, but the words sounded hollow even in his mind. He went into the room next to the one he had first entered and saw that it was much the same—an outer chamber leading to a balcony and a bedchamber within. Both were empty as well, and he again went to the writing desk, hoping to find something of use. There was no stray paper on the desk, and when he went to open one of the drawers his hand was shaking so badly it rattled.

After a moment of blind terror, where he feared the whole estate would come down upon him, he turned and left, returning the way he had come, back into the first quarters and onto the balcony, down the tree and over the wall. He was two streets away before the enormity of what he was doing came to him and he stopped, looking down at his hands. They still trembled violently, and he thrust them into his robes and started walking again.

There were two dancers of the Evening he knew who had paid their debts to the faction that spring and now entertained independently nearby. They would certainly be about at this time of day, and if he was lucky no one would have called yet. He started toward the building where they kept their quarters, hoping they would have some aslyn nectar to help pass the afternoon.

# 3

Keleprai put his second quid of the day into his cheek, hoping it would help dissolve some of the bleariness still fogging his mind, though it was after mid-morning and he had been up for hours. His meeting with Nasyren and Tehh had not helped in this regard, the Adept of Lastl being in an expansive and digressive mood, and Keleprai had found himself discussing the origins of the lilac in the Lastl colors among other arcana. It had been extremely tiresome and of little utility, as many meetings with the Adept were. Now he found himself on his way to an appointment that promised to be even more tedious, if such a thing were possible.

He was heading to the House of Life, where he was to offer sacrifice to the Goddess Melinon. First he would have to listen to an endless sermon by the Sanader of Lastl, a man even more tedious than Tehh. As always, he made the short journey by foot, eschewing the covered palanquin that Nasyren and his guard insisted on. The number of swords with him on the walk had been doubled following the attack, but otherwise he took no special precautions. There had been no signs of any further attempts discovered in the days since the incident, though his agents had spread across the Realm to see what they could discover. Frustratingly little was still known, as his meeting this morning with Tehh had made plain. The meeting he had sent his Disciple to infiltrate had apparently failed to reveal anything of import, which seemed impossible to Keleprai.

His fear, he thought as he made his way from the palace along the Plaza of Remembrance, was that the lack of information was by design. That Tehh could not provide any real intelligence, because to do so would reveal his own guiding hand in the plot. That seemed unlike the Adept, though; given his penchant for subterfuge and deceit, he would have carefully prepared a trail that led any investigation far from him. This conspiracy seemed designed to lead nowhere and to leave Keleprai frustrated beyond measure at his inability to discern his enemy and avenge himself.

The plaza was full of people about their business, all of whom fell to their knees in obeisance at the cries of the herald announcing the passage of the Gver. Keleprai noted a familiar face paying obeisance to him out of the corner of his eye as he passed by, and stopped to call out to him.

"Musician," he said.

The man rose from his knees and bowed in recognition. His name escaped the Gver for the moment, but he had had been playing in court during the Feast of Balance and throughout the city in the following weeks.

"My apologies," Keleprai said, "I do not recall your name."

"I call myself Dathgar, Most Gracious."

Keleprai inclined his head. "Join me for a moment. I'm on my way to attend to a sacrifice."

The musician nodded and fell in beside the Gver. He was small man, strange for someone of Kragian extraction, but he had the long, slender fingers of a musician and a direct gaze that was disquieting.

"I hope that you are enjoying your stay at Lastl," the Gver said, and the musician nodded. "I know that I have enjoyed it. I never hear as much music as I would prefer. I'm told that you are not associated with any of the factions or courts?"

"No indeed, Most Gracious."

"So you have no patron?"

"I have several patrons, Most Immortal," Dathgar said, "all of whom are kind enough to allow me to make my way on the road during the season."

"There are few of the like anymore. Might I ask why?"

The musician shrugged, and again his reply was careful and slow. "I prefer it, Most Gracious. I enjoy the road, seeing the Realm. I hold that dearer than whatever comforts a court patronage might provide."

"You are a figure out of one of the old romances," Keleprai said with a smile.

"I suppose so, Most Gracious."

"Do you know that I once harbored musical ambitions?" the Gver said. They were at the northern edge of the plaza and the gaggle of traffic was halted so they could pass through, the crowds performing obeisance as they went.

"I did not, Most Gracious," the musician said, squinting as they turned east and into the glare of the sun.

"Yes. I was trained on the lute, and the harp of course, and I became fascinated with the whole life. You know the stories one hears as a child. It seemed a life of true freedom. I even wrote some of my own romances. Terrible doggerel, but I was reasonably proficient with the instrument. Then, of course, life interceded."

"Was it not Tysaras—he was of Lastl, was he not—Most Gracious, who was the singing Gver?"

Keleprai laughed. "Yes, that is true. None of his songs survive, if I am not mistaken. Which may be for the best. No, I could force my attendants and courtiers, and whoever else I could wrangle, to listen to me pluck away. I'm sure they would all say I was marvelous as well."

They both fell silent as they strolled along, the Gver lingering to forestall his ceremonial duties. "You look Kragian. Were you born in the north?"

"Yes, I was, Most Beneficent. I came south two years ago."

"So you played there as well, obviously."

"Yes, Most Gracious," Dathgar said. "Some of my benefactors are still there."

"They must treasure your talents greatly. What led you south?"

The musician halted in the middle of the street. "May I impose a story upon you, Most Gracious?"

Keleprai could hear the guard around him move restlessly, but he nodded. "By all means. Speak."

"It is of the war I want to tell of," Dathgar said. "I did not fight in it, of course; I was barely thirteen. But in the year before I came south, I chanced to meet a gentleman who had fought. He was at the battle of Haigah, though he stood against you and Craitol. He told me he was Kercubegahedd's most trusted man, though I do not know that I believe that.

"As I say, I chanced to meet him three years ago. I assumed he was ancient; he was so wizened and shrunk that he could barely move about his home. But he told me he was no older than I during the war. He was like a husk, you know, the fruit having been harvested.

"He told me that he watched on the hill as Kercubegahedd was burned where he stood. He fled and was captured later. An Adept transmuted him with his alkemya, wrenching all his bones, scouring his face until his hair was gone and his eyes were burned from their sockets. And he did other things as well."

"This is dangerous territory you walk on," the Gver interrupted. "You know as well as I the Council's laws on such matters. I am wondering what the tale of a treasonous snake, who stood with the greatest evil that has walked this Realm in my lifetime, has to do with why you came south."

The guard had grown watchful, sensing the emerging tension between the two, and a few shifted their hands over to their swords.

"He is the reason I came south, Most Gracious. He passed two years ago."

"And so? You come to exact revenge? To seek out the Adept who scoured him?"

"No, Most Gracious," the musician said. "I came to tell you. To tell everyone who might listen to his story. Fegh, Usgelt, Devew. They are littered with men like him, wounded beyond any repair. And women. You and the High Adept and our Immortal Qraul all have your songs and your tales, but not them."

"And you aim to give them some?"

"Yes, Most Gracious."

"Tell me," the Gver said, "what do you hope to gain from telling me, or anyone, this?"

The musician grinned, surprisingly. "I don't know, to be honest. I only tell the tale." He shrugged.

A glance from Keleprai and the nearest of the guard had their swords drawn and at the musician's throat. He squinted against the sun, his smile still playing across his lips, fading at the edges. The crowds kneeling around them were careful in keeping their eyes away from what was happening before them, lest they too be arrested and dragged before a court for judgment.

"You had best hope it doesn't lead you to the wheel," Keleprai said, and strode away, leaving two of the guards to deal with the musician, the kneeling crowd scrambling to create a passage for him.

Keleprai's anger at the musician lingered, having festered all morning as he thought about their exchange while the Sanader droned on above the bawling ardeh. This crazed need had seized him to try to recall the man whom the musician had spoken of. It was a fruitless effort and he knew it, and yet he could not relent. He could remember those he had taken to the sword—their pleading faces had come in dreams over the years—but this man could not have been among them.

When he returned to the palace, Nasyren found him immediately, having already been informed of the arrest by the guard. The musician had already been transferred to the Magisterium, and they awaited word from the Gver as to the nature of the charge against him.

"He committed sedition," he told the Master of Offices, outlining the story the musician had told him.

"A very grave offense, Most Gracious," Nasyren said. "Whatever possessed him, I wonder?"

"Who's to say?" Keleprai said. "He may be touched."

"I wonder, Most Illustrious, if he is somehow connected to the attack upon you?"

Keleprai frowned, draining the cup of wine one of his attendants had poured him as he let what the Master of Offices had said sink in.

"There has yet to be any explanation for how the assassin acquired the alkemycal engine after all, Most Gracious," Nasyren continued. "This man has been here since the Feast of Balance, a musician of unknown patronage. There is no chance he came south just to tell you his little tale."

"No," Keleprai said. "Tell the Chief Magister that is where he should begin his questioning."

"Of course, Most Gracious."

"And," Keleprai said, the thought occurring to him in that instant, "do not inform Tehh of this. Be sure that the Magister knows he is to attend to this himself and to speak only to you on the matter."

"Of course, Most Illustrious," the Master of Offices said, his face expressionless as he bowed and left the room.

# 4

These were his only moments alone, where thoughts, let alone aides, were not allowed to intrude. There were guards to be sure, all keeping him within sight while maintaining a discreet distance, and Usen was no doubt within hearing as well, waiting impatiently while his mind ran over the day's courtly duties. So his aloneness was contingent, as all solitude was. One could never completely extricate oneself from the web of ties that constituted a life.

Even the Anchonites, in renouncing all their ties to humanity and heading to the wilderness, trying to create their own sanctuaries, acknowledged the existence of those ties and, in their opposition to them, reinforced them. Or so it seemed to him. He had argued as much with the Imperial Ceinobyte who, bravely for someone so newly appointed to his position, had insisted that the greatest of the Anchonites had reached such a pure form of existence that they had transcended this plain and thus must certainly have severed whatever ties to humanity remained when they had sealed themselves out of civilization, existing with their ear on the pulse of the world. Privately he doubted any such transcendence was attainable, but he had said no such thing to the Ceinobyte. An emperor, ancestors forbid, could not walk in heresy publicly.

He sat under the shade of a gelul tree in full bloom, a type found only in the coastal regions of Luessan. No Ad Eselte had ruled there in over a hundred years. The garden had been built three hundred years before and was populated with plants and birds common to that distant region. At the time of its addition to the private imperial grounds, the gardens of Luessan were in vogue on Nohritai estates throughout the empire, and though they had long since passed from style, even in Luessan itself, the garden here had remained unchanged. In all likelihood, it was the only one of its kind still remaining.

It soothed him to sit here, though he could not have expressed why, smelling the oily sweetness of the gelul fruit that weighed down the spiny branches of the tree. The humidity was less oppressive here under the canopy provided by the trees, and in the morning it was almost cool. It was quiet as well—not in the oppressive way of the Imperial Mausoleum or some other sanctum, but in a way that set him at ease.

He was finishing with the last of the fruit from his breakfast when the Imperial Vazeir, Ibrazol id Ezern, joined him, nodding at the guards as he passed by. He bowed stiffly as they exchanged the ritual greetings, and the Emperor was struck, as always, by the discomfort of the man. He never seemed entirely relaxed in his interactions with others, especially the ritualized ones his position demanded. Yet he was not a shy man, nor a timid one. Something about him moved at odds with everyone else. It was said in court that the death of his wife had changed him in some way, and that before he had been a different man. The Ad Eselte knew differently—the Vazeir was as he had always been, talking as though his teeth were set on edge, moving as though each muscle was braced to face an assault.

Ibrazol sat in the chair indicated him across from the Emperor. Another beside him was empty. He twisted in the chair, looking over to the side, startling a bird as he spoke. "It seems I will not be traveling to Asieren ad Ezern to hunt this season, Most Gracious."

"Events seem to have overwhelmed us," the Emperor said. "You will miss the season."

"Perhaps, Most Benevolent," Ibrazol said with a shrug. "The rains were late in coming. Perhaps they will stay late as well."

"I fear our days will not cooperate even if the seasons do. They are overfull."

The Imperial Vazeir shrugged. "Ancestors will decide, Most Gracious."

So they would, the Ad Eselte, so they would. Each year during the rains it was custom for most of the high Nohritai, and many others who could afford it, to retreat from the heat and humidity of Darrhyn to their paradises. The Ad Ezern, being a desert family, had established theirs on the plain east of the capital, and Ibrazol enjoyed nothing more than hunting the great herds that migrated south with the coming of the rains. The Ad Eselte was not particularly interested in the sport, but he was fascinated by the movement of all these creatures from the eastern plains north beyond Kulez, beyond the imperial border into the tribal lands and their jungles—who knew, perhaps even beyond that—only to return south each year with the season. In the days before the disintegration, before the three kingdoms had broken away, and before the Shadow Men had driven them from the desert, the emperors of Renuih liked to declare that they ruled all the known world. That, he knew, had never been true, and even if it had, how empty a claim when a mere bird flew yearly to parts unknown.

These were thoughts that he was quite certain never came to Ibrazol when he thought of hunting or even animal migration. The Emperor had long ago come to understand that any sort of polite conversation that would pass between them would of necessity be of what he considered to be inconsequential things. In fairness, the other probably felt they were inconsequential as well, but only because he felt all polite conversation was extraneous.

In the early days, when he had first become Ad Eselte, the court gossips had called Ibrazol the hatchet man, the strong arm for the weak-handed philosopher Emperor. Whispers came later, not at the time itself, of the Vazeir's involvement in the unfortunate circumstances surrounding the previous Ad Eselte's—and his father's—death. Ibrazol had not been Vazeir then, merely one of many court functionaries, noticeable only for his military background among so many academy men who found themselves wandering the Imperial Palace under the new Emperor. His rise to Vazeir was all the more notable for the fact that the Ad Ezern had so recently fallen out of favor within the Imperial Government after the escapades of Waleen.

They were not friends, they were too different for that. There were few who knew him better, though, and none he trusted more. Whatever they had was deeper than friendship; a bond of kinship perhaps, or, if the Ad Eselte were willing to admit such a thing, one of need. They had strapped themselves to the same mast and would ride out the squalls together.

They had just subsided to an easy silence when Usen approached, bowing deeply. "Suliher Aths id Negurein awaits, Most Benevolent."

The Emperor gestured for him to be sent forward and Usen retreated, disappearing down the path. A soldier came forward shortly, paying obeisance to both men.

"Jetthir. The desert left you well, I hope," the Ad Eselte said, gesturing for him to sit beside Ibrazol.

"It did, Most Gracious. We had no difficulties."

"What is your report, Suliher?" the Vazeir said, and the Emperor resisted a smile.

Aths inclined his head to the Vazeir. "In summary, we saw nothing that would cause concern. The only Shadows we encountered were clearly families or tribes on their usual migrations. They...well, they did not exactly flee when we encountered them, but they all made sure to keep their distance from us. I would say that they acted as they always do in such encounters.

"We were stalked briefly too, starting on our third night. We never got a clear sighting on who it was, but it was likely just a party from one of the tribes trying to see what we were up to. It's happened before when I've been out there. Once they seem to satisfy themselves that you're not raiding or anything."

"How many groups did you see?" Ibrazol said.

"In the week, Husem—three tribes."

"How many in each?"

The soldier paused, thinking. "The largest was probably one hundred, one hundred fifty Shadows. They weren't all together, though. They were in four or five groups, but moving together, within probably a day's journey of each other. The other two were about half that size."

"And this is usual?" the Emperor asked.

"Oh, yes, Most Gracious." Aths nodded vigorously. "Even the larger group. They often move like that in the larger tribes, with the smaller groups spread out. We followed them more or less for three days just to be sure, but they just went deeper into the desert."

"And there seemed no greater purpose..."

"No, Most Gracious. They seemed just as they always are."

"But that does not mean that the tribes aren't united," Ibrazol said.

Aths shrugged. "That is not for me to say, Vazeir."

"Is there anything you would like to add to your report, Suliher?" the Emperor asked.

Aths shook his head. "No, Most Benevolent. It is all as I have said."

"Thank you, Jetthir," the Vazeir. Aths stood from his chair, bowing deeply to both men before retreating back along the path he had come.

"Well, Vazeir. What say you?" the Emperor said, leaning back on his chair.

Ibrazol frowned. "Difficult to say, Ad Eselte. Nothing appears incongruous. Even the other raids are no different than before. And yet how would we know?"

"I would say an attack upon this city, no matter how brazen and suicidal, signals to me that something is happening."

"Perhaps a new strategy. Though what their goal was I could not say."

"It is troubling," the Ad Eselte said at last, putting a hand to his temple in frustration.

"Indeed, Most Gracious," Ibrazol said. "But nothing so far suggests that the incident was more than an isolated incident."

The Ad Eselte pursed his lips and nodded. "Very well. I would like these expeditions into the desert to continue."

"Of course, Most Benevolent. I will speak to Husem Gheyuth."

He picked up the last of the fruit, closing his eyes as he savored the burst of flavor from the juices. When he was through, he turned to look at the Vazeir. "And our other problem? How are the streets?"

"Quiet, Most Gracious," Ibrazol said. "For now, at any rate."

The Emperor nodded, appearing to be lost in thought.

"We have learned some more, though," the Vazeir continued. "I have a man near the conspirators and I believe that will soon bear fruit."

"Let us hope so. Husem Osiphan is not the sort to sit idle waiting for the harvest to come in."

"We can be certain of the Luessan's involvement, I think, Most Benevolent," the Vazeir said. "A man in our pay was found killed in his quarters four days ago, just after he returned to Darrhyn. A Luessan merchant. He had just informed his minder that he had in his possession maps from the Imperial Survey of the borderlands."

"Disappointing," the Ad Eselte said. "They were not with him, I take it."

"His quarters were ransacked, unfortunately, Most Gracious."

"It would appear that someone has infiltrated our inner sanctum, then."

Ibrazol nodded. "It would seem so, Most Gracious. I have already begun our countermeasures."

"Troubled days with the rains," the Emperor said, the first part of an old saying from the desert. "You will keep me apprised, I trust."

Ibrazol nodded, watching the Emperor's thin fingers now tapping against his cheek. They were hands, he often thought, untouched of anything, pure as the Ceinobytes claimed them. He himself had done things.

# 5

Masiph had already drunk three cups of beer and was onto his fourth when Nazeed found him sitting alone in the drinkery on the western edge of the Uenam. He gave no sign of recognizing Masiph and made a great show of asking both he and the drinkery-keeper for directions to a local academy. Masiph told him that he knew the place well, and after he had sent the man on his way he finished his drink and settled his account. Once outside in the growing shadows of the afternoon almost gone to dusk, he headed for the brothel as well, wondering what Nazeed needed him for now.

Nothing good, he thought, could come of this. In the days since he and Lisser had raided the Luessan merchant's place, his unease at his involvement in the conspiracy had only grown. It had been a relief when Nazeed had not further enlisted him in their work. His thoughts had gained no clarity, remaining murky and fraught with anxiety. In spite of his doubts, in spite of the knowledge that every step he now took with these men would only further seal his fate in the eyes of the Imperial Guard should this insurrection be revealed, he did not stray from his path.

It would be a simple matter. He could go to his father, confess all, and provide what names and information he had and beg for mercy and forgiveness. He would be spared for his treason, but that would be all. Cousin Khibar would become head of the Ad Ezern and Masiph would be disowned in all but name, never to marry, never to inherit, having to live at sufferance of his father and his cousin. Better to be executed for treason, he told himself, though he did not believe it.

When he arrived at the academy, Nazeed was pacing restlessly in the receiving hall, which was empty but for the bawd, who was careful not to look at either of them.

"We don't have much time," Nazeed said as he led Masiph through the twisting hallways of the brothel to the alley behind, and from there to the gnarled byways that surrounded it. "We have to be across Uenam by nightfall."

Masiph did not reply, nor did he say anything when a covered palanquin materialized on an empty street and, after they had slipped within its confines, began to carry them farther to the west. He knew better than to ask what they were about, especially with the ears of the carriers so near. Instead he settled back into his seat and put a quid in his cheek, hoping the aslyn would shake off the drowsiness he felt from the ale he had been drinking. Nazeed paid him no mind throughout their journey, staring off into the palanquin curtains, lost in his own thoughts, which only made Masiph more nervous. It was unlike him; normally he was quick to set the youth at ease.

They switched palanquins several times in their journey, exiting on one empty street and following a circuitous route set by Nazeed to another quiet avenue, where a palanquin awaited their arrival. In this way they gradually made their way to what Masiph recognized as the eastern edge of the Uenam, where Nohritai families of middle rank had their estates. He did not understand the abundance of caution Nazeed was using, given that they could both reasonably account for their being in the area without issue. Unless he was worried about them being followed, but who would know to follow them?

By the time they reached their destination—an unremarkable street near the Uenam Walls—night was falling and the lamps were in the process of being lit. Masiph thought he recognized the street they were on, though he could not be entirely sure in the darkness, but they did not remain there long, Nazeed leading him immediately to the servants' paths that ran among the various estates. They were all unlit, though Nazeed had no difficulty finding his way among the many alleys. As they went along, Masiph caught snatches of conversation from the gardens of the estates they were passing, all unremarkable and yet somehow ominous because of that.

Finally, after many further twists and turns that left Masiph confused as to where exactly they were—having never used the servant paths himself—Nazeed drew to a halt before an estate, small even for the area, and slipped within through the servants' door, which had been left unlocked. They moved quickly across the insubstantial though immaculately maintained gardens, to the main house, where Nazeed went unerringly to the third window, which had been left unbarred. They crawled in through that to a darkened room that Masiph, squinting against the shadows, thought was an aslyn room. It was small enough, the low table was there and he could feel the sitting rugs beneath his feet.

There they remained, crouched on either side of the door, for what seemed like hours to Masiph. The hallway beyond was dark as well, and the house seemed quiet, though Masiph strained at the slightest sound of activity. The family, he surmised, must be out for the evening and the servants gone to their quarters. Which meant a long wait.

He had nearly fallen asleep, the beer settling in him, when the sound of footsteps approaching started him to wakefulness. A glimmer of illumination followed the steps, growing brighter as the sound came nearer. Glancing across to the other side of the doorway, Masiph saw that Nazeed was gesturing furiously at him to rise. After staring at him uncomprehendingly, the ale making him stupid, Masiph mimicked Nazeed, standing up and pressing his back against the wall near the doorway. Another gesture from Nazeed told him that he was to stay against the wall when the man entered.

The footsteps came to a halt just beyond the door, and the light from the lantern danced as whoever it was raised it up to look about the hallway, as though to ensure he was alone. Nazeed stepped away from the wall and sat at the aslyn table, gesturing again with his hand for Masiph to stay where he was. The door opened a moment later, light flooding the room, causing Masiph to blink, and a Nohritai stepped within. Seeing Nazeed, he nodded and went to the table to sit opposite him, setting the lantern on the table between them.

"Is that wise?" Nazeed said with a gesture at the light as Masiph closed the door and barred that path, standing with his arms crossed.

"I am not going to stumble about in my own home," the man said with an imperious wave. He glanced toward the doorway, noticing Masiph for the first and nearly jumped to his feet, his face going white with fear.

Masiph felt the blood drain from his own face as well as he stared at the man and realized that he knew him. He was a trade administrator in the Vazeir's Palace. *Ancestors save me*, he thought, *I am doomed*. Nazeed, he saw, was expressionless, glancing from one man to the other as though waiting to see who would act first. After a moment, Masiph managed to master his emotions and stared levelly at the two men.

"What in ancestors' name is this?" the administrator demanded, bringing his fist down hard on the aslyn table, shaking the lantern.

A smile tugged at Nazeed's lips. "Are you trying to rouse the whole house? What would Husem Ruleth say if he found us here?"

"The old fool," the administrator began to say before stopping himself and adding more quietly, "State your business and let us be done here."

"Very well," Nazeed said. "We have concerns about the other night with our mutual friend."

"The Luessan? It was exactly as I told you."

"Was it now?" Nazeed said. Masiph felt his breath go still in his chest at the mention of the dead merchant. What had gone wrong, he wondered.

"You would know better than I," the administrator said, a note of unease entering his voice, though his demeanor remained haughty.

"Yes, I would," Nazeed said. "Your man was seen."

"What are you talking about?"

"Do not pretend with me. The boy was there," Nazeed said, gesturing at Masiph, "and he saw your man."

The administrator, disdain clear on his face, turned to look Masiph over as though he were the lowest of plebeians. His expression vanished in a second as he recognized just who Masiph was and whirled to face Nazeed again.

"What is the meaning of this?"

"I warned you how far our reach was," Nazeed said, even as he reached across the table and knocked the man senseless with his dagger.

The administrator sprawled forward, knocking the lantern over, spilling the oil and flame onto the floor. Masiph, the ale still slowing his thoughts, watched as Nazeed frantically gestured for him to smother the flames while he subdued the administrator. It was only when the putrid smoke reached his nose that he reacted, taking his outer robe and throwing it upon the flames. As Nazeed dragged the still-unconscious administrator from danger, Masiph righted the lantern and stamped on his robe to extinguish what remained of the fire. It went out quickly, though the smoke remained, stinging their eyes and nostrils.

"Quick now," Nazeed said, waving away the smoke and handing Masiph his dagger.

Masiph stared down at the blade in his hand, the weight of it now disturbing, though he had held any number of similar weapons before. He turned to look at Nazeed, a question on his face.

"Cut his throat," Nazeed whispered to him. "Quickly. Someone will smell the smoke before long."

Masiph looked doubtfully from the administrator to the blade. "Why?"

Nazeed seized him by the shoulders, looking directly into his eyes. "He recognized you here tonight. You saw it as well as I. And he betrayed us. He gave us the information about the Luessan, but he had someone there to see who was there to do the job. He was planning to betray us. He cannot be allowed to live."

"How do you know there was someone there watching us? I didn't see anyone. Lisser didn't say anything. You said I saw something."

"Lisser saw nothing as well. We have another man in the Imperial Palace; more than one, in fact. He informed us that this whoreson had gone to those above him, telling them that he knew who had killed the Luessan. If he lives, he will certainly reveal your involvement. Your father will know. We cannot risk it. You cannot risk it. You must kill him. Quickly now, before we are discovered."

Masiph nodded. He knew Nazeed was right. Even if he was lying about the man knowing about his involvement in the merchant's death—Masiph had thought he looked surprised to see him—there could be no doubt the man was aware of his involvement now. It was a test as well, he knew. Nazeed wanted to see how far his loyalty would take him, to bind him more fully to their cause. And this would absolutely. Would Ibrazol even spare him the charges of treason were he go before him begging for mercy his hands covered in blood of the man from the palace? Doubtful.

These thoughts flickered through his mind in an instant, time slowing to an agony, as Nazeed shoved him to where the administrator lay. Masiph crouched over the man, fingering the dagger, his mouth dry. His eyes burned from the smoke and he could feel the itch of a cough in the back of his throat. The dagger was poised in his hand but still he hesitated, unsure how to do this. Did he have to, he wondered? There must be another way.

Voices from somewhere else in the house disturbed his reverie. Below him the administrator stirred, blinking his eyes and coughing at the smoke.

"Cut his throat," Nazeed said, anger in his voice. "Before we're discovered."

The sound of footsteps approaching and someone calling out, "It's in the aslyn room," spurred him to action, adrenaline blotting out any further thought. With a vicious motion, he drew the blade across the man's throat, causing his eyes to fly open and a cry of surprise to sound. Whoever was approaching gave a shout and started to run toward the room. Masiph watched for a moment as the administrator struggled to breathe, air escaping out his throat in red bubbles. He plunged the dagger into the man's chest for good measure.

Nazeed was already gone out the window and Masiph stood to follow him, only to find that the administrator had hold of his arm and was rasping bloodily, trying to call on whoever was approaching. Masiph kicked himself free, leaving the dagger behind in the man's chest and his burnt robe on the floor, and tumbled out the window. As soon as he regained his feet, he started to run, plunging without heed through the garden to the servants' door, where Nazeed awaited him. Behind him he could hear shouts as the alarm was raised.

Nazeed embraced him, as though they were brothers now, and they both ran, Nazeed leading the way, to an empty street where a palanquin awaited them.

# 6

Usyre id Reteln ys Luzyren moved imperiously through the kitchens of the Reteln estate, issuing instructions with each step, emphasized by a sharp gesture of her hand, her daughter and two eunuchs following in her wake. Every so often she would stop and turn to Nyzrella to elaborate on some order she was giving to the servants.

"It is important," she said, stopping before a shelf filled with jars of spices and bunches of dried herbs, "to get in the habit of looking over the spices. Perhaps once a week."

"You can get your castulan" — she gestured at one of the eunuchs who stood at her side — "to do so as well. In fact, he should do so more often. And the head chef as well. But making the habit of doing so yourself helps to ensure that they are doing their work as they should. And never forget the value of the things. A handful of jesten can fetch five kenir."

Nyzren watched as her mother opened each jar and peered in to check its level. A wave of odor passed her way with the prying away of each lid, an almost intoxicating mix. As a child she had loved to come to these shelves and smell the contents of the various jars. Kenul, the chef, would lift her up so that she could reach the higher ones and inhale their scent. She could not say what it was that had fascinated her about the aromas of food, especially of the spices. It was not just the pleasure of eating, the coming sustenance their smell indicated—there was something more to it. Even then she had understood somehow that all these spices came from something else, somewhere else. When she was a bit older she would ask Kenul to describe to her what plants each spice came from, what they looked like, where they could be found.

"Nyzrella. Pay mind," Usyre said, sharply breaking her reverie. With a sigh she turned from the spices and followed her mother on through the kitchen.

Usyre continued, telling Nyzren what she should have her castulan do, what she herself should do, what those in her kitchens should do. The expense of this and how to ensure the servants did not steal from her. Her husband would expect her to keep the kitchen staff and the women's quarters in line.

Kenul approached them, bowing to Usyre and smiling at Nyzren. She smiled in return, ignoring her mother as she complained to Kenul that they had been going through too much fowl lately. It was expensive, regardless of the type of bird, and a certain economy was needed in preparing it for dishes. Kenul nodded gravely in reply.

Nyzren remembered once coming into kitchen late one night, perhaps on the day of a celebration, only a few servants still about the kitchen cleaning up or eating the leftovers. Kenul had been preparing his own meal while he supervised those still left. She remembered noticing the exhausted satisfaction on his broad face at a day's work done well and had marveled at it. He had not asked why she was still about, the guests all gone and the household in bed, nor had he sent her back to the women's quarters, where she should have been at that time of night.

Instead he had let her watch as he fried up some kuull, river shrimp, with garlic, tomatoes, and dried chilies. These, he had told her, were his favorite food growing up. Perhaps even now. He let Nyzren try one when he had finished them, for Usyre did not allow plebeian food to be served at their tables. It was a remarkable thing, firm yet tender, almost dissolving as she chewed it. They were difficult things to cook well, he told her. If you didn't cook them enough, there was no firmness to them. If you cooked them too much, though, they became tough, all the moisture leeched out of them. They had to be fried at a high heat to ensure that they kept their shape, but that of course meant that they cooked fast, so there was only a very short period where they were done just right before they were ruined.

Those fleeting moments when the kuull was perfect, those were what you lived for, the chef had said. They were there and then gone and you spent the rest of existence trying to regain them, only to lose them again.

"Pay mind, child," her mother said again. "Have you been listening to a thing I've said this morning?"

"Of course."

Usyre frowned, looking doubtful. "You are fifteen, Nyzrella. By the end of this summer you will be betrothed, ancestors blessing. In a year you will be married, ancestors grant us, and in charge of a household of your own. If you don't learn this now you will bring shame to this family and your new one."

Nyzren nodded, refusing to meet her mother's eyes. Usyre shook her head, waving a hand in exasperation, and led them out of the kitchen. They returned to the women's quarters where Nyzren's rooms were, along with her mother's and her grandmother's. Her grandmother, she felt sure, would insist on conducting similar tours of the household, dispensing the same kind of wisdom in her certainty that her daughter-in-law did not know how to properly run a household. And her mother would be furious that she was being undermined yet again. Bad enough that Osiphan confided more in his mother than her—that woman sought nothing more than to poison her daughter against the Ad Luzyren.

"You must be firm and strict," Usyre said, "especially when you first enter the household. After a time you will know which of them you can trust, which will inform on you, and which are useless. But strictness is the key with eunuchs. Even the few you will be allowed to bring with you. They should not be your confidants. They are your servants, just the same as the servants they are charged with."

Nyzren glanced at the castulan, Tequihan, and thought she saw him trying to stifle a smile. She was having difficulties herself, hearing her mother talk of strictness with eunuchs. As long as she had been aware of such things and privy to the gossip of the household, her mother had had a eunuch as a lover. That eunuch she would dote on endlessly, giving him gifts, allowing him to escape all duty. She had always wanted to ask her father about what he thought about the eunuchs, whether he had spoken to Usyre about them. He had to know about them, didn't he? It would not be the eunuchs that would bother him, she suspected, but the flagrance with which his wife carried on with them. He was a man of circumspection in all things.

After lunch they were to go to see some of the Luzyren cousins for an afternoon in their aslyn room, but when it came time to go Nyzren begged off, claiming that she felt unwell. Usyre looked her over suspiciously, placing a hand on her forehead to feel the temperature, but eventually she relented. "Perhaps it's safer that you stay home anyway, things the way they are," she rationalized.

Nyzren had not even felt angry upon hearing that, as she often did when her mother sought to keep her within the walls. Better here than chewing with her cousins all afternoon.

"Stay in your rooms," her mother said before leaving. "Don't let me catch you in the gardens. You might really come down ill if you stay in the sun and heat."

When her mother had gone she sent Quesin, her eunuch, to the library to bring her a book, and then went to the gardens. He set out a chair in the shade for her and brought her some fruit to eat while she read. The book he brought her was the lessons of the Sage Nuerrallah, one of her favorites. Her father had taken her to his mausoleum two years ago, a day's journey east of the Darrhyn, and she had made an offer and composed herself before his tomb, prostrating with a few others. Then he had let her tour the women's sanctuary and talk with some of the Ceinobytes.

She remembered all of it: the silence of the mausoleum, the placidity of the sanctuary, the smell of sage and wild grasses and flowers on their journey to Luisel, the town that held the mausoleum. The palanquin they had taken had been enclosed, as any palanquin carrying a Nohritai woman had to be, but Osiphan had allowed her to peek out through the curtains and stare at the passing countryside. The sight of the plains' expanse, an endless horizon beneath an empty sky, had stunned her. She had not thought that the world could seem so large. She had looked at the slight rise of the hills in the distance and realized that she had probably never before seen so far. The sky looked larger, a brighter shade of blue, dwarfing even the grasslands.

*Ancestors brace us, guard us, guide us to the highest plains. Purity, the unity of all form, is possible in this world. Do not let others suggest differently. Belief, earnestness, humility…*

She stopped reading, her thoughts distracting her. She felt a slight pang of guilt at not going to see her cousins. Byriele was to be married later this summer and would likely want someone to commiserate with.

She recalled her mother's own words this morning. Married within a year. The thought made her want to weep. Before she might have, but now she simply pushed it aside. She refused to pity herself—it accomplished nothing, and she had only so much time left and she did not want to spend it in pointless misery.

She had seen too much of her mother going through her empty days ordering servants or disappearing to be covered in scented oils by her eunuch to look forward to marriage. The thought of ordering a household and going to chewing rooms and being cloistered in the walls of some other family's estate appalled her. She could accept it here, though she chafed against the restrictions placed upon her, but somewhere else, under someone else's law.

When they had returned from Luisel she had asked her father to let her join the sanctuary as a Ceinobyte, to live a life of purity and contemplation. He had refused, of course, though she thought there might have been some pain in his voice doing so. She was his only daughter, and since she had only the one brother, she was very necessary to the family. She had known that and still she had asked, hoping that somehow he would not be able to deny her.

It began to rain. She had not even noticed the clouds passing over. She handed the book to Quesin, who hurried inside with it and the fruit. She rose to follow him but stopped instead, letting the rain drench her. She stayed watching the rain fall, small puddles forming that would be gone by morning, breathing in the aroma of the damp grass, the sweetness of the wet earth, her skin tingling as the raindrops crashed against it.

# 7

*Everything is pure, nothing is pure.* So the great sage Nuerrallah had said, a sentiment that had passed so close to the Enir heresy that his teachings had been banned in the empire for nearly half a century, his followers forced to worship in secret, keeping his tomb only surreptitiously. Only in the last few decades had his doctrine gained any credence beyond a small cult of outcasts, even penetrating the elevated circles of some of the better Nohritai families.

One of those who had embraced the teachings of the sage was Osiphan id Reteln who, after the birth of his first daughter, had become much more dedicated to belief. In his readings of various sages, both ancient and more recent, the one who had spoken most plainly to his feeling of the world had been Nuerrallah. It was perhaps coincidence, perhaps not, that soon after his conversion he began his drift toward opposing the Ad Eselte and advocating for Nohritai rights, a passion that had only grown as his family had been excluded from post after post across the empire.

Nyzren knew that her father was conflicted on the subject of her own belief. On the one hand, he loved that his eldest daughter shared his passion and faith, for his wife and brothers did not. They were satisfied with merely offering grace to their ancestors and little else. But her desire to enter a sanctuary in one of the Nuerrallite orders was something he could not allow, and she often thought that he must have wished she did not share in his faith, for he knew the burden on the heart to stay of the world.

He had told her once, "We have no choice but to be of the world and to live as unified a life as we can here in this realm, and to hope for the grace and blessing of our ancestors in the next plain that we might be granted the chance to follow our desires."

He knew her suffering. He knew. *Everything is pure, nothing is pure.* She read the words again. More than anything, she wanted to follow the sage to the wilderness, the northern plains of the empire, the edge of which she had glimpsed on her journey to Luisel, where he had lived in solitude in the midst of those great herds of which she had only read. She knew that was beyond anything she could hope for, no woman had ever done such a thing that she was aware of. Still she often dreamed of it, the feel of the wind on her face while she lost herself in a reverie and waited for a true understanding to come over her and cast her free from the burdens of this life.

The Shadows were attacking Darrhyn under the cover of night again, coming this time in untold numbers, flooding over the city walls, the Watch helpless to stem their tide. As quickly as they appeared they dissolved into the city, lying in wait for their moment to strike. Nyzren knew where they were going, but she was helpless to do anything. It was to the Walled City, where the Nohritai, the flower of Darrhyn, lay helpless and asleep, trapped upon their estates, including her own family.

The creatures emerged from the darkness, attacking the estates of the high and powerful, laying everything to ruin. Nyzren could hear them enter her estate, though she was unable to raise any alarm or even attempt to flee, her terror overwhelming her senses. Screams from elsewhere in the house told her that her mother and her eunuch lover had been butchered in the bed where they lay entwined. Her father was not there; she could not say why exactly that should be the case, but she was certain it was true. Where was he?

She did not have time to dwell on this, for the Shadows were soon swarming her room. She felt feverish, an overwhelming heat stultifying the room, and she wondered if they had set the house to flames. They did not put her to the sword, at least not at first, as they had her mother. She lay there immobilized with terror beyond anything she could imagine while they each set upon her, one after the other. A strange exultation came over her as they defiled her, the agony and degradation transmuted somehow, a revolt against all that held her to this realm, even as she still wanted to scream and scream until her lungs were ragged.

After a time, when the Shadows were through with her and the looting had begun, she found herself floating through the Walled City, drifting out beyond the river and swamp, past the thin stands of forest, to an infinite plain where a great herd of some magnificent unknown creatures stood in the distance. She found herself returned to flesh then and joined them, moving as they moved through the days and seasons beneath that vast endless sky. Everything is pure, nothing is pure.

Nyzren awoke to find her body heavy with sweat, yet she was shivering as though she had a fever. When her trembling had subsided, she flung off the covers to her bed and leapt out of it to look around the room and see if there were any Shadow Men about. There were none, of course, as she had known there would be. A dream and nothing more.

But when she closed her eyes, the Shadows were still there, coming one after the other, all intent upon her. She felt her breath coming quick in her chest. *Ancestors forgive, ancestors forgive me*, she mouthed to herself again and again. Her flesh was in revolt against her soul, her senses defying her thoughts. She would not think of it. A dream and nothing more.

She was so distracted that it was some time before she realized that there were voices coming from outside. She froze, panic momentarily seizing her again, and then crept closer to the window, taking care to stay below the sill, though there were curtains over it and whoever it was would certainly be standing on the ground below. One man's voice was distinguishable, which meant he must be standing directly underneath. The other was too low for her to understand, though she thought it might be her father. Something about the voice, his intonation, but she could not say for sure.

The one she could hear said, "He said they had no problems, although she was still there when they came and demanded more coin."

There was what she thought was a question from the other man. The first replied, "Yes. It was exactly as we were told."

The other man spoke for a long time, and she strained to make any of it out, but it was of no use.

"Yes, I will see to that immediately." There was a small pause and then he said, "Ahednar sent a message today, through safe channels about our man in the Vazeir's Palace. Apparently we are brother darrhynna in his nest."

There was a sharp response from the other that she almost made out. She thought she heard the word *truth*. She was now even more certain it was her father.

"He would not tell me unless he was certain. Apparently he had someone watching that morning. The boy will be recognized."

Another question followed, and the man replied, "No, but he is working now to find out. Once he does I think I will see how true the boy's loyalty is."

She waited for a further response but all she could hear was the still of the night and her own breathing.

# 8

The night was still heavy with moisture, although the day's rain had long ceased, the air in the streets immovable as the buildings. In the drinkeries and other establishments still active in the late hours, there was a sluggishness to the activity, strange even for Darrhyn, as though only somnambulists were about. There was a hesitancy, a waiting to everything, as though some spark might shake the heat from its grasp of the city.

It was something of a surprise, then, to the drowsy revelers when the Imperial Guard appeared in force on the streets in certain neighborhoods across the city. Rumors of their being on the march traveled moments behind them, and many of the lights that dotted the cityscape blinked out at their passing. A warehouse in Luithen was the first place the Guard struck, seizing all those who were gathered. From there they spread across the city to houses, drinkeries, and other places where similar gatherings were being held, beating and arresting those who were there. There was little resistance, for the Guard struck without warning, catching nearly everyone unawares. Only at the Dravasyl, a drinkery in Hueithel, did word of their marching reach the assembled before the soldiers, in the form of a breathless Nohritai, who had narrowly avoided being seized at a minor sanctuary, having been late to join his gathering. Those not involved immediately scattered to the winds, but those who had taken the cause, assuming their names had been betrayed, determined to make a final stand.

They lasted most of the night behind the barricaded doors, the Guard reluctant to burn them out. The proprietor, a sympathizer, had allowed them to use the upper story of his establishment for meetings and storage, so they had a small cache of bows on hand. With those and some pots of scalding water, they were able to keep the force opposing them at a distance, killing nearly dozen of the Guard while losing only a handful of men. Toward morning, though, as their supply of arrows dwindled, the Guard managed to find a large enough ram to take out their barricades and it was all over very quickly.

Those who survived, and they were few—some had taken daggers to their hearts rather than be captured—were hauled to the Yuehilth, along with the rest who had been arrested that night. In years to come, the disaffected among the Nohritai would speak of those who had fallen against the Guard that night as martyrs to a greater cause, of which they were a part, though the cause itself would prove more fluid. Any number of insurrections, minor or otherwise, in the decade that followed were taken in their name, and though the Empire sought to stamp out any cult around them, shrines in sanctuaries in Darrhyn and elsewhere were dedicated to them. Their graves—for even the Ad Eselte would not tempt the wrath of their ancestors by denying the Nohritai a proper resting place—became sites of pilgrimage and worship, taken in secret, and the songs and tales of their deeds grew out of all proportion.

In the ensuing days, the Imperial Guard set about finding whoever they had missed in their first sweep of the city, as well as collecting anyone whose name passed the lips of one of the prisoners at Yuehilth. By the third day, nearly three hundred men had been arrested, with another forty having been killed. The city was in a state of frenzy by that point, with talk of bands of Nohritai planning to storm the walls of the Imperial Palace and rumors of plots to poison the waterworks or rupture the canals. When the Guard halted their incursions into the city and no uprising or violence had occurred after the fourth day, a measure of calm was restored. The moment, it seemed, had passed.

The executions, which began the next day, only served to bring an even greater sense of finality to the events for the majority of the populace. There were a few public executions for those said to be the ringleaders, while most took place in the Yuehilth. The crimes of all those who had been arrested were announced at the beheading and scrawled on posters that were nailed up in public squares. Most of the dead ended up on the city wall, their torsos speared on a stake, on top of which was placed their severed heads, the mark of a traitor to the Emperor carved on their faces. A few others were thrown into cages that could be found in most squares. For a fortnight the stink of death gripped those places, and then the bodies were taken down and the defiled remains returned to their families. They were Nohritai, after all, whatever treason they might have committed.

By and large, most of those involved in the conspiracy were Nohritai, with a scattered few from other walks of life sprinkled into the mix. Nohritai in name, as it was said, for most were career officers and administrators, or distant cousins of important families. There were one or two sons involved from families that the Ad Eselte knew he could not simply arrest and have killed, and these were dealt with quietly—not so quietly that those in higher circles did not know who they were, though, and that was a point in itself. The development that truly shocked the high Nohritai was the placing of the Ad Reteln estate under the command of the Imperial Guard, which resulted in a stream of higher families making their way to the palace to pay obeisance to the Ad Eselte, carefully distancing themselves from that family.

The make-up of the insurrectionists meant that the populace was more or less indifferent, once it became clear that the Imperial Guard would not be marching the streets every night hunting for prey. They are always playing these games, it was said, and it was no concern of theirs if the Nohritai decided to slaughter each other. The Nohritai were divided in their opinion: there were those who supported the Ad Eselte and other families who were sympathetic to the cause, but for the most part it was treated as one of those unfortunate incidents that occurred from time to time in the Empire. There would always be petty Nohritai who resented their lot and families who opposed the Ad Eselte, and sometimes that opposition would lead them down such a path.

The days returned to their regular order following the executions, those who might wish to avenge them seeming to understand that the opportunity for any action was past, at least for the moment. The streets had their usual clamor, and, if there was still talk about the incidents of the last days, it was in a way that suggested something long done. The bodies on the wall were ignored; there were always bodies on the walls, after all, though few wearing Craitolian silks.

TWO:

THE PASSING OF DAYS

# 9

The earth was copper colored and hard, covered in scrub and rock. What vegetation there was did not come past his knees, mostly a twisting labyrinth of brambled brush. Donier picked his way through it, his eyes on the long horizon, the sun beginning its descent to his left. He walked with a purpose this time, as opposed to the others, though it was not immediately apparent where he was headed.

There were mountains behind him, jagged monstrosities of shadow glowering in the sun. He was in the same valley as always, its end still not apparent, somewhere at the glimmering edge of the horizon or beyond. The sky was clear and the sunlight heavy, but he felt no heat and his feet were light on the ground.

There was no one with him and no creature stirred anywhere in the sky or across the vast plain. It was all silent but for the wind that whistled down through the valley, stirring the scrub in his path.

Never, as far back as he could recall, had Donier suffered troubled sleep. He rarely could recall his dreams. By the time he emerged from the mists of unconsciousness, they would have drifted away, leaving only pieces in his mind, a half-remembered image he could not quite bring into focus. And now this, a dream, the same in all nearly all its details each time, that came every two or three nights. Sometimes, as now, he would awake, and other times not, but he would, no matter when he woke, be able to remember the entirety of it, as if it were a mosaic crafted on a ceiling.

Ulternon of the Hall, it was said, sent messages to the chosen through dreams, for sleep was a kind of death. Nothing, Donier thought, would seem to indicate that he—second of a cohort of Lastl, middling son of a middling family—would ever be chosen by the Gods. It was not at all clear what the God was telling him, either. What did his being lost in the desert, empty of Shadows, indicate?

Thinking of the creatures made him think of Terainous and then, inevitably, Liene, asleep in her crypt of a house, and he realized that no amount of turning would send him back to sleep. He got out of bed, washed his face in the basin, dressed, and left his rooms, not bothering with a candle. There were the beginnings of light stirring below the sky in the west, so he had no trouble making his way down to the kitchen, where the cook and his servants were already busy.

A fire was burning hot in the oven, and by habit he went to stand and watch the flames, though the day promised to be hot. There was a pot already sitting above the fire, flames dancing up to lick at it. One of the servants brought him a cup of dala sweetened with honey, and Donier thanked him.

"A hot day I think, Nes Donier," the cook said as he passed to put something else over the fire.

Donier nodded but did not reply. It felt as though his mind would never still. A child started to wail upstairs—his son, who had just started teething and had been miserable this last week. Jullavin, after his grandfather, Jullavin Donevyr. The second son born to him by that name, the first buried last year at the age of two, gone to Hall from fevers.

The wet nurse managed to quiet him eventually and the calm of the morning returned to the estate, the oven's fire and the subdued hum of the workings of the kitchen the only things to disturb the peace. Donier left them and went out to sit in the courtyard. The shadows were long and the darkness still heavy beneath the trees of the gardens.

His father was there already in those pooling depths. His knees had begun to bother him these last years, so he was up to walk every few hours. Lately, with the dreams they had been passing each other in the halls on these nightly sojourns, neither disturbing the other's solitude. Donier did not do that here either, sitting beside Jullavin as they each finished their cup of dhala and watched the sun rise.

The last days, since his meeting with Uherl, had been ones of torment, filled with constant glances over the shoulder while on crowded streets. The past, safely buried, had not remained. It had sprung forth through the cracked earth and now threatened to blossom into a poisoned fruit. A sort of doom seemed to mark his steps now, just like those of his dreams. This was fate, though—the Gods granted them the illusion that they controlled their days, but it was only a bittersweet reverie.

All their days were covered by that looming shadow, easily ignored, until one day it was not, one day it was there to be faced. Terainous had faced it that day by the river and it had broken him. But for the Gods' chance Donier would have faced it years ago as a member of the Veil. Instead, he had dealt out his fate to others, only to be faced with it now again. How easily a path was turned, though they all were well trodden, leading to the same place.

He glanced over at his father, wondering if Jullavin could sense the anguish his son was battling this morning and hoping not. He had aged so much these last few years that he was nearly unrecognizable from the man Donier had grown up with. Always a quiet man—he had become nearly mute in the last year—there were days when he did not speak at all, and he would spend hours in the courtyard watching the changing of the day while his sons managed the affairs of the estate.

Sitting here with him now, Donier envied him this luxury of time and silence, letting the days pass in view with his eyes open at what was to come.

# 10

Alieren, Qraulla of the Realm and wife to Laterala, stifled a sigh as one of her ladies announced the arrival of her husband to her bedchambers. He had been to her rooms every night for the past fortnight, and it had been like their first times together with Laterala driven by a furious urgency. What lay behind this burst of vigor she did not know, though she suspected it originated from either the High Adept or the Master of Offices urging their charge to get his wife with child. His time was upon him now, apparently, though why that should be she couldn't say.

It was worthy of further attention, though, and she had set various of her agents and allies at finding out what they could. She had known the High Adept was planning something from the moment she had heard of the assassination attempt in Lastl. Why else would the man have gone in secret to visit the Gver if not to set in motion some scheme of theirs? As yet she had discovered nothing, beyond the fact that the attack had been a very near thing indeed.

Laterala had been unusually closemouthed when she attempted to extricate some information from him, which either meant that something very important was going on or that he had not been informed of what it was. Most likely both, knowing the High Adept. Laterala was such a boy still in some ways, she thought, still so impressionable and easily swayed. It was just unfortunate that the High Adept was his guiding light. That man was dangerous, as she well knew, being from the north and having seen the ravages his kind had committed.

She rose to her feet as her lady left the room. She always received Laterala in this manner, as if she were standing guard over her virtue, though it had only ever been his. In truth, she did not mind his increased attentions; if nothing else, it gave her more time to bend his ear and try to steer his course against the winds prevailing upon him, but his valor often outran his consideration for the prize he was claiming. He did not greet her as he entered the room, leaving the door for her lady to close, taking her into his arms roughly, his mouth at her ear.

"Is your altar ready to offer your sacrifice?" His hands were already at the workings of her gown.

"So long as it is a bloodless one. That time is long passed."

He laughed, and she helped him as he removed her robes and then his own. He moved to seize her once again, but she stopped him, grasping his arms.

"Aren't you going to offer your prayers before the altar? It is a divine sacrifice, after all."

"So it is. The Gods themselves know it. I am Qraul of all Realms, though, do not forget, and all must kneel before my throne."

"Don't I always," she said, her hands firm, "I'll go to that paradise once your devotions are through."

He lay next to her when they were finished and she listened to his breathing as it settled, feeling his chest expanding and contracting. He made no move to leave, and she put a hand on his stomach, running her fingers along his contours absently. He was in a rare mood this evening, clearly. Was he this way with his doxies, she wondered? It seemed likely; he would not blame them for his lack of heirs—though as far as she knew, and she had seen that it was investigated thoroughly, none of them had gotten with child either.

That she had not was still seen as a failing on her part, proof of the cold blood of northerners and their essential weakness. She had heard endless whispers to that effect, and some worse, in her three years here. People were always watching her, at court, in the hallways of the palace, as though if they stared long enough they might discern the reason for her failings. For a time it had weighed on her heavily, there had been sleepless nights and tearful breakdowns for no reason when she found herself alone with her ladies. She shuddered now even to think of it.

Laterala had been the worst. He had blamed her, of course, accusing her in one moment of being a salamander, frigid as the northern winters, and in the next of betraying him with another man. Never mind that one of the Master of Office's eunuchs shadowed every step she took all her days within the palace. It had been ugly and he had treated her as though she were the commonest of harlots those first months, until one night he had been too much in his drink and struck her in the face as they argued. That had proven a step too far, and Alieren had summoned all the hurt, all the loneliness, all the resentment at the accusations that had simmered below the surface, and she had ordered him from her chambers and refused to see him until he apologized.

Cowed by her fury, he had gone, nearly fleeing the room, Alieren remembered with a smile, and she had at last understood that she was not entirely powerless, not just a vessel for the Qraul's child. Cepedutherupt had been incensed at her actions. That had been their first confrontation, though not their last. The High Adept had threatened her and her family with unspeakable consequences if she did not submit, but she had refused, and finally, after several icy days, Laterala had come before her and begged for forgiveness.

From that moment on their relationship had been transformed, and if he did not love her, as all the songs said, she certainly had his respect and his ear. One of her agents had even told her that the Qraul's predilection for northern girls had begun after their conversation. Alieren was not sure what to make of that. All she knew for certain was that he would listen to her counsel now. She had managed her own triumphs in the intervening years, though the spoils had been meager. It had been enough to feed her soul and keep her from privation.

Laterala stirred beside her, shaking her from her thoughts, and rolled, kissing her ear.

"What thoughts tonight, my love?" he said.

She smiled at him. "You have a secret."

"Do I?" he said with a frown, his tongue still attending to her earlobe.

"Yes," Alieren said, playing with a tuft of his hair. "You have been far too quiet lately."

"I have been too much at prayer."

She laughed. "I have heard your invocations. They are most pleasing."

"I am glad," he said, moving to kiss her neck and shoulder.

She sighed and said, "I would hope that you see me as your counsel-keeper and would share with me what is taking place within your Realm."

"Of course," he said, smiling his maddeningly innocent smile, and kissed her hard, his mouth closing over hers and then wandering down to her breasts, and she caught her breath.

# 11

Keleprai sniffed the air judiciously, as though testing the various notes of must that were heavy in the air. He looked at the cascades of books and scrolls and various other scratchings and wondered how Tehh accomplished anything. There were uneaten meals lying in the strewn rubble somewhere, he was sure. That was the only explanation for the smell that clung, not only to the Adept's quarters, but into the hallways beyond. The rain that morning only added to the smell of decay and parchment. His head began to throb, because of the smell he was certain, not helped by the fact he had not slept in the last two nights. This had to be punishment for some grievous wrong he had committed, he decided; there was really no other explanation for the sort of misery he was feeling at the moment.

The Adept shuffled into the room, the cup of dala now retrieved. Probably days old, Keleprai thought, suppressing a shudder.

"I presume, Most Gracious," Tehh said, having settled himself in his chair, "that you will be wanting an update on our investigation."

"Indeed."

"Very well." He took a sip from his cup. "Hieran, as you will likely know, did not see Ussul enter the house, nor either factor, for that matter. It is possible that they suspected their letters were being read."

"This was what, ten days ago?" Making his impatience plain.

"Eleven, in actuality, Most Immortal. I am setting the scene, you understand. The players are arranged and now we can proceed. We have gone forward on the assumption that they know we are reading their letters and watching them. They've been very quiet, though, very quiet. If the head factor has left his estate, we have not seen him."

"Perhaps his son was sick after all."

Tehh looked baffled.

"Didn't Hieran say that he was told he could not go to see him because his son had the fevers?"

"Ah. Of course, yes. That is right. It would be a very long illness if that were the case," Tehh said.

Keleprai studied the Adept carefully. He wasn't sure whether Tehh was dissembling or whether he had actually forgotten that detail. He had always been a difficult man to read. There was something about this, though, that felt wrong to him, and had ever since Nasyren had revealed that Tehh had known Cepedutherupt was at Lastl.

"What about the player? What was his name?"

"I don't recall, don't recall. Not important, though. We haven't been able to find a trace of him. He's dead, I would hazard, if the people we're dealing with are intelligent. And everything would suggest that they are."

"So what now?" Keleprai asked. A challenge. He had told Nasyren to conduct his own investigation, since his meeting with his wife and everything that he had heard from that to this point suggested that there was no link between the Avellar and the Apysel. And it made sense to him: Ussul was not such a fool as to be seen on the streets with the men he was conspiring with.

Tehh sighed loudly. "I think we are at an impasse, frankly. I will have my people continue watching the factors and reading their letters. But I suspect the moment has passed and we'll get nothing out of them. They won't be doing anything to attract suspicion now, and they've cleaned up all their messes."

*Yes,* the Gver thought, *someone has had time to clean away all evidence of guilt.* There was also the matter of alkemycal engine, and how the assassin had come into possession of it. As yet, the musician had revealed nothing to the Chief Magister, but Keleprai was certain that was where the connection lay.

"What about the engine?" he said to the Adept. "Do we have

any information on how it came into the hands of the assassin?"

Another sigh from Tehh, as though the matter troubled him deeply. "No, I am afraid not. It is a matter of grave concern, obviously, if the Apysel should prove to be in league with the remnants of Kercubegahedd's forces. But I suspect the man was just an assassin for hire. Many of Kercubegahedd's followers have turned to such work to survive."

Keleprai nodded. It was what he had expected the Adept to say—it was what he had been saying all along. Briefly he considered revealing the arrest of the musician and hinting that the man had begun to reveal his connections to see what reaction Tehh had, but he decided to wait and see if there was fruit to bear on that tree.

Instead he turned to the other reason he had decided to suffer the Adept's quarters. "We have other matters to concern ourselves with," he said. "We have been summoned to Craitol."

"For what reason does our Most Illustrious Qraul require our presence?"

"Recent events to our east have concerned him. The fall of the pyrsedy, the riots in Takyl, and of course the raids."

"It would seem to me that these are internal concerns, matters for yourself and the Gver of Takyl to handle as they see fit. It is not as though the Shadows are an imminent concern."

Keleprai nodded. "Our Qraul has determined otherwise."

"I see," the Adept said, touching a finger to his craggy cheek. "I see no purpose to my going if it just to be a discussion of border matters. The result is always the same. More men in the pyrsedies, more patrols. And none of it will stop the Shadow Men."

"I don't know what our illustrious friend intends. He has called for a full Council of Gvers, and Cepedutherupt has summoned the Adepts as well, so you will get your say."

Tehh sighed again, and this time it was not an affectation, or at least so it seemed to Keleprai. He shook his head. "He will not rest until he has his war with the Shadows."

Keleprai inclined his head, knowing he was talking about the High Adept now, although he did not say anything.

"Where do you stand on the matter?" Tehh said, raising an eyebrow.

"I think it is folly. I have told him as much."

"As have I," the Adept said with a shake of his head. "He is set on it and nothing will turn him aside, I fear."

"He has overreached here, I think," Keleprai said. "If a war is truly what he intends, the other Gvers will not stand with him. Especially not with Apysel to rally to. All this Council will serve is to bring the dissension to fore and weaken the Qraul."

"It is a delicate time to be attempting such a war," Tehh said.

"Hopefully we can help him see reason on the matter. If not, Pervelte will see to it."

"If it is left to him there will be blood," the Adept said.

"Given what has happened so far this season, I fear there will be regardless," Keleprai said.

Tehh looked as though he was about to say something else, but he took a sip of dala instead, looking past the Gver.

## 12

It seemed to Nyzren as though the estate had undergone a sudden and cataclysmic metamorphosis. An incomplete one as well, for no butterfly had yet emerged from the ruins of the caterpillar. She could not shake the sense, as pervasive as the silence that had draped everyone and every room since the Imperial Guard had come, that she now inhabited an ancestor-less tomb, unkempt and abandoned by the living. She had hardly strayed from her rooms these last three days, fearful of what she might encounter. How long had she raged inwardly at her entrapment in the women's quarters and her rooms, and when the moment finally emerged that she could wander the estate at will, she was unable to?

Not knowing was the worst of it. No one would tell her why the Guard had come or what they intended to do, aside from making them prisoners in their own estate. She had demanded that Quesin tell her what was going on, but all he would do was sadly shake his head, which only served to enrage her. Osiphan must have instructed him and all her servants to tell her nothing, there was no other explanation. She had struck him in the face the day before when she had asked him and he had again refused to say anything. He had lowered his eyes in submittal, and she had horrified herself by hitting him again before running from the room sobbing.

The thought of it even now caused her face to burn with shame, and though she tried to console herself with the fact that her blows could not have hurt him, that they had not even left a mark, she knew that was hardly the point. Her entire realm as she knew it was crumbling, but instead of the tumult or chaos she might have expected in its wake there was a stagnation, as though the passing of days had slipped by their estate, leaving them to obsolescence. She had awoken the night before unable to breathe, the force of it all pressing against her chest.

Today, though, she had resolved not to be ensnared by fear. She would trust in her ancestors. She would remember the words of the sages. This was existence for now, and she would have to learn how to live within it.

Both Osiphan and Usyre had sequestered themselves in their respective quarters for the last three days, and neither of them would see her. One of her ladies, who had come from her mother's people, had spoken with them on the day the Guard had come. She had been told that Usyre had taken to her bed in despair, not even allowing her favored eunuch to see her. Her mother did this often, refusing to see anyone or even eat for days, usually when she was angry with Osiphan or his mother over some perceived sleight.

Nyzren could only imagine what she was feeling now. The Ad Luzyren had always made it a point of pride to be in favor with the Ad Eselte. That was why the Reteln had wanted the marriage with Usyre for Osiphan. The blow to the family's honor was beyond recovery; they were forever marked now with this association. How long before the Ad Eselte trusted their name again? Even Nyzren knew that much, no matter what happened in the days ahead.

She was determined, though, that none of that would affect her, she would go about her day as always. *Married within a year.* These were the last days that were nominally her own, where she could maintain the illusion that there were chances and choices that might change destiny. Ancestors knew it could not be other than it was, though, especially since they would need her marriage more than ever now.

Quesin frowned when she told him she was going to take her breakfast in the garden, but said nothing. He brought her a chair and some food and a cup of dala, setting everything up in the shade of a lime tree near the house. Nyzren would have preferred to be further into the gardens, away from the estate house and the claustrophobia of its walls, but she understood his reasons. It was pleasant outside, the usual heat absent but the sun still bright and the sky clear. It looked as though it would be that rarest of days without rain. She savored the taste of the fruits Quesin brought and the pungency of the limes above, trying to forestall thought and just exist in sensation.

After finishing, she got up and walked deeper into the gardens, seeking to escape the shadow of the mansion. Quesin cleared his throat uneasily, but followed. The estate had a series of small gardens behind the main house separated by walls of vegetation with a winding path that led one through it. There were open spaces where one might host gatherings or hold games, and at the farthest end a canal that connected them to the Aesen canal, the central waterway of Uenam. A stream had been constructed to run off it that wound its way through the estate. She headed for the canal, as it was a place she always enjoyed. There was a bench near the boathouse that looked out on the canal that she liked to sit on. From there one could see through the grated gate out along the canal's path as it connected to the larger waterway.

When she came near the boathouse, though, there were two guards standing nearby, with others likely on the outer side of the gate. Of course there would be, she thought, of course there would be. She stared at them, unsure what to do. Why hadn't she thought of this before? One of the men noticed her and turned to stare, his face expressionless. She could feel a flush creeping into her own, and though she knew he would not be able to see it, she was still furious. She wanted to appear as unaffected as he.

"Come Husem," Quesin said at her side. "We should go back."

He was right, of course, but still she wanted to refuse to go and sit on the bench and make a pretense of looking out on the canal in spite of the guard. That was foolish, though, and she knew it. The only thing that would accomplish would be to start rumors about her decency and perhaps force her father to do respond in some way to assure the family's honor. She turned, as gracefully as she could manage, and walked back, Quesin behind her, hoping that it looked as if this had been her plan all along. She understood now why her mother and father were in their rooms. Her hands were shaking and her legs felt weak. It was such a violation. To be stared at as though she was nothing more than a creature one kept in a cage.

Once inside the main house, she felt relief flood over her and hated herself for that. She dismissed Quesin and he went, though he looked as though he wanted to stay with her. Left to her own devices, she decided to go to the kitchen to try to glean some information. Kenul was sitting at a table near the back, writing his usual list of things that needed to be bought at market that day. His greeting, she thought, was nervous, although perhaps that was more her looking for any signs of distress to match what fluttered in her stomach.

"You have decided to rejoin the realm, Husem."

She smiled. "Yes. The air was getting a bit stale."

"I should say, Husem," he said, returning his attention to the parchment. She sat on a stool across from him, looking around the kitchen. The only times she could remember it being so quiet was after a funeral. Normally it was raucous with noise; not just the clanging of dishes and the sizzle of food in pans, but the shouts and jests of Kenul's assistants. Often she would find him at the center of a flurry of activity, singing to himself above the fray.

"Do you know, Husem," he said to her, gesturing at the parchment, "that this is the first food I will have been able to bring in? Ancestors' grace we have the gardens, or I don't know what I would have done."

She asked him directly what he had heard about why the Guard was here. He looked uncomfortable, and she thought he was going to refuse to answer.

He sighed and set his quill aside. "Poor Husem. None of us knows really, though I would guess your mother and father have means of getting information, Guard or no Guard."

She wondered how that could be when no one was allowed entrance or exit, but she said nothing.

He hesitated before continuing, "But talking to one of the guards—we're feeding them, you know, feeding our captors—and he did tell me a bit." Another pause. "They say that there was an uprising. Or at least the plannings of one. But they were found out, and the walls, he said, are lined with bodies. I don't know. He would not say much."

"Why are they here, though?" She knew the answer without hearing it, but she wanted to have it said.

"Husem Osiphan was involved. The man would not say how. Likely as not, he may not know, Husem. But he was involved."

"He must have been one of the leaders," she said, but Kenul did not reply. "What will happen?"

The chef shrugged. "Who's to say, Husem? I am only a chef,

not a Vazeir. It cannot stay like this forever, I would say. Something will have to happen. Ancestors grant that it is quickly."

Later, thinking it through in her rooms, she realized that nothing could be the same now. Even though she had known that, it had not been real to her in some way. She had thought that somehow things would return to normal. They would have to. They were the Ad Reteln, after all; this would pass with some blow to the honor that her mother would agonize over, but which would ultimately mean nothing in the larger plain. But seeing the Guard and hearing from Kenul what she had already suspected made it more tangible to her. Her father had committed treason against the Empire, and if that were the case then it did not matter how important and powerful the Ad Reteln were—the Ad Eselte would have to do something. It could not stand.

Would they execute him? She went cold at the thought. Exile, perhaps. She did not know enough of the history of the Empire to know what happened in these sorts of instances. The other Great Families would not allow one of their own to be executed by the Ad Eselte, even one who had committed treason, would they? She didn't think so. And yet what argument could they make, and why would they, unless they supported Osiphan's cause? She understood why Kenul had prayed for a quick resolution, whatever the result, for the true anguish was in not knowing what was to happen.

The rest of the day she spent in her rooms, moping and restless. She dismissed her ladies and Quesin. The silence bothered her, but their refusal to discuss what was happening was so infuriating, when talking of anything else was unimaginable, that she decided to bear it. She didn't feel like reading or keeping up her diary or any of the other things that she would normally do to pass the time. Instead she just lay on her bed thinking about their captivity until the weight of it became unbearable.

After eating that evening, she decided she had to do something or she would go mad with all this energy and thought and no outlet. Unable to think of anything else, she went to the library, thinking that she would read the lessons of Nuerrallah. Her father was already there doing the same. He smiled distantly when he saw her.

"Come for this, I imagine," he said.

"I don't know what I'm doing here, actually."

He didn't seem to hear her. "I know I always find it such a comfort. I read this and I feel as though I have done right by my ancestors."

She sat down across from him as he returned to the tome's pages. Watching him, she felt like she was intruding on a private moment and wondered if she should leave. She decided against it. He had had nothing but privacy as far she knew these last days, and if he wanted her to leave he would let her know.

He looked up finally and favored her with another distracted smile, running a hand over his balding head. "Don't worry," he told her. "There is nothing to fear. The Guard will not be here forever. They answer to the Ad Eselte."

"What will happen?" she asked, not knowing what kind of answer to expect.

He thought for a moment before answering her. "There are many possibilities as to what happens next. Nothing is so bleak as it seems." He smiled. "Ancestors favor us, no one knows what the next days will hold."

# 13

Vyissan was a prisoner in all but name. *Honored guest*—the words brought a wry smile to his face. Once he revealed his letter, he was at the mercy of the Ad Eselte. Or in this case the Imperial Vazeir, the Emperor's proxy, the Emperor himself little more than a rumor to this point. He tried to imagine how they would treat a Renian in Craitol, but he knew it would be much the same. A secret imperial emissary, whose provenance had to be accepted, and whose goals were unclear. To say nothing of how the nobility or the populace might react if they knew of the emissary's presence. No, they had no choice but to lock him away until they determined what to do with him.

Not that it made the waiting any easier. Vyissan sighed, rising from the bureau where he had been trying to write, and began to pace his quarters. He had exhausted everything that he might say this last week to the point that he was now simply tired of his own thoughts and words. A solitary existence was preferable only if one had chosen it, not when it was forced upon you. And not when those outside these rooms held your fate in balance. Could fair Melinon reach him in this godless realm, he wondered, not for the first time?

It was a fine prison, he had to admit. A six-room prison, a number he knew the Enir at least considered auspicious. There were the two rooms of his bedchamber, the study he had just been in, a dining area where he took his food and two rooms near the entrance for receiving guests. He headed there now to see which guard was standing watch over him.

He was disappointed to find the older of the two soldiers. A thoroughly disagreeable man, taciturn and clearly disapproving of Vyissan's presence within the palace walls, he had spoken no more than two words to him over the past eight days. The younger Renian, who alternated with him, had been reticent initially as well, but boredom had proven to be too much for him and the last three days he had talked a little with Vyissan.

Yesterday he had explained that these rooms were actually quarters for the wife of the Vazeir, which explained the ample space. When Vyissan had asked why he had been given them, the guard had eagerly explained that the Vazeir had no wife. She had apparently died some years ago in childbirth, the fourth of four sons. At this the guard had made a warding sign.

"They say it was a true love match between them," the guard had said.

"A rare thing."

"Oh, indeed. I should say. Such a tragedy for him to lose her in that way. Do you know the healer who attended blamed the child? Not that it helped him," and he drew a line across his throat.

Tragedy, it seemed, had stalked the Vazeir, his three eldest sons perishing while in the army. Vyissan was unsurprised by this. The Vazeir seemed a hard man from their meeting, and here was probably why. There was a violence lurking behind his exterior that he could not entirely hide. When they met that first time, the Vazeir receiving him in a spartan room near his audience chamber, it had taken a great deal of will on his part to stand his ground. The Vazeir wanted him to reveal his purpose, and the purpose of the Realm in sending him, but he refused, saying he was unwilling to trust any intermediaries to deliver the message he had for the Emperor.

The Emperor, he was told, was at his paradise and would be for an undetermined time. "For your purposes I am the Ad Eselte," the Vazeir said. "If what you have to tell me requires a decision of consequence, then word can be taken to him. But I am his ears and his tongue while he is outside Darrhyn."

Vyissan smiled. "I understand, of course, but I will await his return. I am pressed by our Most Immortal Qraul to deliver these words to his ears alone."

They went back and forth with such niceties for a time, both of them smiling and gracious until, realizing that Vyissan was not going to reveal anything, the Vazeir relented. "As I say, I cannot give you a date when the Ad Eselte shall return. In the meantime, you shall be our honored guest. I will give you some rooms in my palace here for your stay and some members of my own personal guard for your protection. If you require anything at all, we would be happy to help you."

It was not a request, and Vyissan was led from the audience to his rooms by two armed men. That had been eight days before. The Vazeir had been to see him once since then, perhaps hoping that he would be more in a mood to speak. He had no idea if the Emperor had returned to the city in that time, or when he intended to. The Vazeir had refused to discuss anything around the state of affairs of the Empire, and even the talkative guard fell silent on these matters.

For all he knew, the regime might be in its last days, the Emperor having fled the city to escape a rebellion. From the windows of his quarters, Vyissan had seen an inordinate number of soldiers making their paces in the last days. Whether this was normal or not he could not say. If it was out of the ordinary, it certainly could not be solely in reaction to his arrival. Perhaps the Vazeir himself was planning something and wanted to know what the Qraul of Craitol intended before he enacted his plan. There was no way to be sure the Emperor even knew he was here.

This was his lot in life, to suffer the decisions of others and to wait for them to be made. The Gods had given him this burden; he had been entrusted with this task and now he had to see it out. Still, he thought of the walk across the desert and the journey upriver— how simple it would have been to turn aside at any moment and wander off into a new existence. How wondrous to slip off these shackles.

The claustrophobia of these rooms, the path he was wearing on the floor, combined with the worry, were beginning to wear at him, he decided. At some point he could no longer wait for events to lead him—he would have to act. In the meantime, he would need to speak with the young guard at every opportunity.

# 14

"Are you trying to drive yourself into a life of squalor, Husem?"
Ctuellan said, acid on his tongue, as he cleaned up the remains of
the previous night's meal, which consisted of several dishes of
picked-over food and two empty bottles of wine.

Masiph chose not to answer the question, turning away from
the eunuch. His mouth was dry and thick from the wine, though
his head, thankfully, did not hurt.

"Husem, you will need to leave your rooms at some point."

He ignored that as well, though he winced when Ctuellan threw
open the curtains over the window, letting a shower of light into
the room. After a day yesterday when it had been somewhat cool
and dry, it was unbearably hot and the air was heavy with moisture.
It was really all quite unbearable at the moment, he thought
morosely.

Ctuellan had brought some pastry and a cup of dala, which he
put on the table, the smell reaching Masiph as he roused himself
from the bed. He grabbed the cup, leaving the pastries, and went to
stand by the window. It looked down on a garden that saw little use
with a weathered fountain at its center, a tribute to some forgotten
Ezern. He nearly pulled the curtains closed, but then changed his
mind, deciding to bear the light; his eyes pulled up to the
mausoleum dome catching the sun.

He had been in his quarters the last three days—or perhaps
four, he could not remember—hardly eating and pouring through
bottle after bottle of wine. He had not yet drunk enough to suitably

dampen his fear. For a time it would be chased away, but it always rallied, rushing back, a tide growing strong.

No, it had been four, he thought as Ctuellan busied himself with making his bed, four for certain. He had been on his way to meet with them, had stopped off at a drinkery because he was too early, and after his last evening with Nazeed he had required something to steady his nerves. Someone had come in just as he was nearing the bottom of his cup and called out to everyone that the Guard was on the march, arresting Nohritai. There had been a great deal of chatter as people debated what and who they were out for, and in the midst of that he had slipped out and fled down the streets home. And he had not yet left.

The arrests had ended and they were on to the executions now, or so one of the eunuchs had said the other day. Masiph was still surprised he had not been detained yet. Now everything was dependent on who the informants were, who had been seized, and who had talked. The eunuch told him several hundred had been captured, but surely some must have escaped.

"Your father would not approve of this," Ctuellan said as he collected the remains of last night's meal. "This is not the way for an Ad Ezern."

One of the few blessings ancestors had granted him these last miserable days was the absence of his father from the estate. Ibrazol was staying at his rooms in the Vazeir's Palace, had been for over two weeks now. Obviously he had been preparing this strike against the conspirators and now he was handling the clean-up. At some point he would return, and then, Masiph thought, there would be a reckoning.

It made him ill just to think about it, and he longed for some wine instead of the dala Ctuellan had brought. He leaned against the window, running through various scenarios of informants and turncoats. Which prisoners had spoken under the press of the wheel? Had he somehow left evidence of his presence at the administrator's house? He thought not, but it would not matter. Nazeed had been there. Between he and Lisser Masiph could easily be tied to two murders, to say nothing of what would happen if Husem Osiphan decided it was in his best interests to reveal the involvement of the son of the Imperial Vazeir in his conspiracy.

Inevitably it would be; he would be a chip to barter in exchange for leniency, or just to exact a small measure of vengeance against

Ibrazol. What a fool he had been. This was always how it had been going to end, waiting for the sword to descend, and he had no one to blame but himself. His hands began to tremble as he stared out the window.

He hated himself for this endless fear, this bounded existence where all he faced were walls. Even sleep offered no succor, for all he saw when he closed his eyes was the startled face of the administrator, surfacing to consciousness as his throat was slit, his cries of agony still resounding in Masiph's ears. The night before he had awakened to his own screams, though thankfully he had not roused Ctuellan or any of the other eunuchs so far as he knew. How long before he incriminated himself in his slumber, his dreams forcing his guilt to the surface for all the estate to hear?

"This cannot continue, Husem," Ctuellan said as he left the chambers, giving Masiph a stern glare as he said it. He stared out the door after the eunuch had left for a long time. Yes, he thought, somehow it would end, and he shuddered. He walked away from the window, set the cup back on the table, and returned to bed.

# 15

The cook Kenul fidgeted nervously under Osiphan's gaze, the deep olive shade of his skin edged with white, the blood draining from his face. Osiphan tried to ignore his own anxiety and to project only calm, authority and normality. He was simply a Nohritai giving orders to one of his servants, nothing that had not happened a thousand times before without either of them giving it a second thought. Now, though, the thought was there between them, unspoken, which somehow made it even more visible to both of them.

"Who among your staff do you trust without question?" Osiphan said again to the cook.

Kenul shrugged his shoulders uncomfortably. "I do not know, Husem," he said. "They are all good sorts. None of them steal."

"Think carefully," Osiphan said. "I have a message that I need carried and your staff are the only ones allowed off the grounds."

"The Guard will search them, Husem."

Osiphan tried not to let his frustration show. Kenul would never have acted in this manner before their house arrest, he would not have dared to hint at defiance, but now he knew lives and honor were at stake. Osiphan was not even certain he could trust the cook not to inform the Guard, but he had no choice but to rely upon him and his staff. His own people he trusted absolutely, but the Guard would know not to let them through. Someone had to be sent, though—he could not wait another day without news. Who had been arrested? Who was left? Who had betrayed them?

"Baush, then, Husem," Osiphan said after some consideration. "He is the cleverest of the lot. He will know what to say to the Guard if they question him and he will be able to memorize the message easily."

"Send him to me," Osiphan said, and returned to his quarters to wait. An hour later, Htiaga, his eunuch and castulan, ushered the youth into his presence. Osiphan looked him over with a critical eye, noting with approval the deferential look on the servant's face, as well as the obvious intelligence glimmering in his eyes as he took in everything looking about the room.

"Are you prepared to accept this burden for this family?" Osiphan said.

"Yes, Husem," Baush said.

"Good," Osiphan said, and proceeded to tell him what he wanted him to do. He was not at all certain the gambit would work, as there was no way of knowing who had been arrested. His only hope was that Nazeed had managed to escape, which he was confident was the case. The man could hide in plain sight, and the Guard would be looking for a Nohritai man.

The two of them had planned for an eventuality like this; one had to. If Nazeed was still on the streets then he would know to go to the markets where the Ad Reteln servants were likely to be. And if Osiphan wished to contact him, he would send a servant to a specific stall with a specific request. Nazeed could then intercept the servant and messages could be passed along. There was still danger to it. The servant would almost certainly be followed by someone from the Guard, but Nazeed was skilled enough to make contact on those crowded streets without someone following the servant being the wiser. It was just important that Baush keep his head.

Osiphan judged him a sensible youth, and he repeated the instructions he had been given flawlessly, so he sent him on his way and waited, trying not to let the anxiety overwhelm him.

Baush was followed as he made his rounds, the imperial agent doing little to disguise what he was about, ensuring that he kept the Ad Reteln servant in sight at all times. The youth went to the fruit stand near the new shrine to the Sage Yulateh, in that cluttered and busy corner of the market that had been rebuilt after a fire six years before. He asked for a kastril, a fruit from Elen that was out of season, and, after being denied by the proprietors, made his way from there through the crowded ranks to the butchers, where there would be fresh ardeh, fish, and chicken for sale.

It was difficult for the agent to follow Baush through the press of the crowd, so his eyes were drawn forward to make sure that he did not lose sight of him in the warren of streets and stalls, and he did not notice as a short, somewhat fat man slipped alongside him. He was only there momentarily, just long enough to slip a dagger into the man's side. By the time the agent realized what had happened and started to look about for the culprit, Nazeed had already disappeared within the mass of people about their days and he was falling to the ground. It was several moments before his collapse drew the attention of the passing crowd and by then he was already dead.

Having assured himself that there was no one else following the servant, Nazeed made contact with Baush, and they talked as the youth made his way among the butchers selecting the day's meat. Neither of them lingered, Nazeed vanishing into the crowd and Baush hurrying back to the Ad Reteln estate.

Osiphan listened to what the youth was saying with a pained expression, his eyes closed and a finger touching his temple as though his head ached. The news was all grim. It seemed nearly everyone had been caught up in the raids the Guard had carried out. They had known the names of nearly all involved, as best Nazeed could tell, and worse, had known where and when they would be gathering. The only logical conclusion was that there were informers in their midst.

The obvious candidate was Nazeed or Lisser, given the breadth of their knowledge of the operation, but Osiphan dismissed them out of hand. Lisser, according to Nazeed, had been executed. As for Nazeed himself, it was simply beyond belief that the man who had stood beside him for all these years, before the conspiracy had even been a glimmer in their eyes, could have betrayed him. It did not bear thinking about, he told himself.

"He says you should not try to contact him again," Baush said. "There is too much risk. He will find a way to reach you."

Osiphan nodded and dismissed him. The servant bowed deeply and left the room, leaving him alone with his thoughts. The only glimmer of hope—aside from the fact that Nazeed was still about on the streets and organizing what assets of theirs remained—was that their man in the Vazeir's Palace still remained undetected. There was a weapon that could still be used to strike at the whoreson Ibrazol, who, Osiphan had no doubt, was behind the ruin of all his plans and dreams. That and the boy. *Imagine the look upon Ibrazol's face,* Osiphan thought, *if I told him.*

There was more troubling news from their man in the Imperial Palace. It seemed an emissary of the Qraul of Craitol had arrived. No one was sure what the ancestor-less, alkemya-worshiping scum could be after, but Osiphan was certain no good could come of it. The Ad Eselte was not someone guided by the Sages. He would put little store in the sacred principles of their ancestors. Osiphan was certain he would invite the Craitolians in with open arms if they offered him a few baubles and the promise of a better hand to be played with the three kingdoms.

He cursed again that fate and his ancestors had not granted him the opportunity to see the Ad Eselte's reign at an end, that the whole realm would be left to suffer under his faithlessness. There was little left he could do, he thought, but at least he could see that the emissary was given the reception he deserved. Beyond that he could only hope that his ancestors smiled upon him at last and that Nazeed was able to produce a miracle worthy of the Sage Nuerallah.

# 16

Masiph's fingers were still greasy from the chicken he had bought at one of the stands in the Flower Market as he made his way through the city to the eastern wall near the Jessin Gate, where the executed were displayed. His stomach registered its displeasure with the speed at which he had eaten the fowl, worried as he had been the entire time he stayed by the stand that someone might notice him. He wiped his hands clean on his robes, not caring as they were smeared with grease. It would help him look the part. He had decided, and now regretted the choice, to wear common robes instead of his usual Nohritai dress in the hopes that he might better escape notice as he made his rounds through the markets. Instead he was still left feeling exposed, with the added worry of determining how he might explain himself should someone recognize him.

So far he had been to all five squares where the executed were being displayed in cages. He made his way among the market-goers, trying to see who was among the dead without appearing to be looking, a far more exhausting enterprise than he had expected. Mostly this was because of his constant fear that the Imperial Guard would materialize around him to lead him away to Yuehilth, though he told himself again and again that if they intended to arrest him they would have done so already. Surely they knew where to find him, after all.

He rushed through the streets without heed of others, mostly out of a desire to be done with this, but also in the hopes that he might be home before the afternoon storms erupted. It looked now as though he would be thwarted in that desire, and he muttered at his inability to rise from bed at a decent hour, to say nothing of his procrastinating through most of the morning. Whatever courage remained in him he summoned, because this had to be done. He could not go another day not knowing.

The execution wall was full of bodies and crowds of flies and birds working at the corpses. The smell was overpowering, even as far below as he was. It was only when faced with the sight of them that the enormity of what he had been involved with became apparent to him. So many of the faces were as young as his own, Nohritai dissatisfied with the lot life had cast them and too impatient to accept it. Most of them had probably known as little about what they were doing as he, their only treason passing messages for their masters or drinking with the wrong sorts. There but for his ancestors' grace went he.

He walked down the entire stretch of bodies and then back again to make sure he did not miss any of the faces, marred as they were by birds and the marks of treason on their foreheads. There was no sense, he realized, in disguising what he was doing here. No one stopped him, though, or even gave him a second glance. Apparently it was not uncommon to spend one's time walking the wall here—hardly surprising given the number of executions in a city the size of Darrhyn.

Most of those he had associated with had not known who he was, nor he them, so he felt no worry as he passed familiar faces. There were only a few in particular that he was looking for. One of them he saw on his second pass through, a familiar grimace contorting his lips. The last time he had seen that was when they had gone their separate ways as the morning took hold of the sky after their raid of the Luessan merchant's apartments. Masiph felt ecstatic seeing him up there, and he stared at him for a time, trying to suppress a smile. Either Lisser had not known whom he was, which seemed hard to credit, or he had not talked.

He left the wall feeling light and exultant, laughter burbling in his throat. Somehow he had escaped. Nazeed had not been among the dead and Masiph was not sure how he should feel about that. Osiphan, he had decided, he could trust to keep his counsel. The Ad Eselte could not execute a high Nohritai, and it would be useful to have someone like Masiph, who had emerged unscathed by this disaster and who would owe him. But the fat man...who knew where his loyalties would direct him.

It did not matter. He had walked the streets, he had seen the bodies, and he would walk the streets tomorrow again. The rain began, slowly, a steady drumming building up as the heat of afternoon heaved and exploded open. He was soaked through, the wool of his robes heavy and itchy against his skin. He wanted to sing.

# 17

The days grew increasingly desperate for Vyissan as they passed with no word from anyone as to his fate. He began to wonder if perhaps the Vazeir would just save himself whatever trouble Vyissan was bringing by having him killed. Imagined scenarios filled the waking dreams he found himself in, the enforced stasis of each hour leading his mind to continually wander down such trails, all of them ending somehow with Nesyur's face contorted in a rictus of shock, blood spilling down his robes.

There would be no knife for him, not at first—the imperial torturers would apply their instruments to see what could be learned. A terrifying thought, for no matter how many times he told them the truth they could choose not to believe, to resubmit him to the rack or the wheel under the conviction that one more turn would send his secrets spilling forth. They did not believe he was from Craitol, he suspected—they thought he was an agent from one of the Republics, or even from within the Empire itself, sent to carry out some plot.

Vyissan could not blame them for that belief. How long had it been since an emissary of the Qraul had visited the court of the Ad Eselte? Over twenty years, someone had told him before he left. There was a reason for that. Craitolian emissaries had a habit of being killed in Darrhyn, because most emissaries were also Adepts or at least practitioners of the alkemycal arts. The Renians' revulsion to the art was legendary. And yet here he was, putting his fate in their hands. A more foolhardy thing he could not imagine.

The soldiers no longer marched outside the palace, at least not in view of his windows, so perhaps the difficulties, whatever they might have been, that had developed upon his arrival had now passed. He thought that a positive development. Perhaps now the Vazeir would listen to his claims without suspicion marring his eyes. Vyissan doubted that—the Vazeir was not a man to ever be at ease in front a stranger like himself.

How was he to convince them that he was what he claimed to be? Reveal his true shade? That would certainly provide proof beyond all doubt that he was from Craitol, but it might very well destroy any trust in his intentions at the same time. What man of good will traveled hiding his true self? He had been told that Renians suspected all men of Craitol to be Adepts, even those of northern shade, which was why he had disguised himself as an Enir, to avoid that very suspicion while on the road. It had served him well enough there and had helped to gain him entry within the Imperial Palaces. Now, though, events moved beyond his orbit.

The Gods offered him no guidance, though he had given blood to Melinon. There was only waiting and trusting in the Vazeir, the man who held his fate in his hands, and the Gods. They had given him much kindness in the time he had been allotted; perhaps they would see fit to grant him a little more.

It was in this state of the mind that he faced the Vazeir, who returned to speak with him again nearly a fortnight after his arrival. He was accompanied by a servant, who brought a tray with a bottle of wine and a box of quids. These were set on a low table as the Vazeir greeted Vyissan in the Renian manner, clasping wrists and embracing cheek to cheek. They sat on the rug across from each other as the servant set out a spittoon and a candle and a bowl filled with belet leaves.

"You are familiar with the aslyn ceremony?" the Vazeir asked him.

Vyissan inclined his head and took a leaf from the bowl as the candle was lit. He had shared this ceremony with several Enir before in Craitol, and when it came time for the invocation he did not call on his ancestors but the blessed Melinon and Senteur to provide him guidance.

He complimented the Vazeir on the quality of his quid, a truly exquisite mixture. The growing buzz of the aslyn did nothing to quell his nervousness, though the sharing of the ceremony seemed to indicate a thawing in relations. The servant poured a measure of wine for each of them and left them alone. Vyissan noted that the talkative guard had left them as well.

"The Ad Eselte has returned from his paradise," the Vazeir said, all ceremony dispensed with. "I spoke with him yesterday about your presence and your desire to share an audience with him. He has agreed to hear what your great Qraul has to say."

"My humblest thanks, Husem."

"We have not yet determined when; there is much for him to deal with at the moment, you understand. But it will hopefully be in the next few days. He is most eager."

"And I am most eager to meet his excellency and hope that he will be pleased with what our Most Beneficent Qraul has to say."

The Vazeir spat. "I ask your patience a little longer and apologize that it has taken so long. I hope that you and your Qraul will understand that it was a result of necessity and that we meant no disrespect. These are troubled and difficult times."

"All times are, Husem, and these especially."

"Quite so, quite so." The Vazeir spat again and then rose, bidding Vyissan farewell.

Vyissan exhaled, the weight of days of fear falling off his shoulders. Now at last the end was in sight. Though not entirely—what would happen once he revealed what he was? He could not forget that either. This was Renuih, after all, and his life would very much be at stake. The lies within his lies of which he would slowly have to unburden himself. They had become as much a crutch as a weight upon his shoulders these last weeks. He took a sip a wine to calm the itch growing at the back of his mouth.

The servant returned, snuffing out the candle and taking everything but Vyissan's half-finished cup of wine. He watched him go and then stood alone, unsure what to do.

The next morning, restless after his meal, he wandered out to see if the talkative guard was on duty. His name, Vyissan had discovered, was Hasen, and he had been a soldier in the army before becoming a member of what they called the Imperial Guard. He was not of noble blood, yet he was already a man of rank, however insubstantial at the moment, and clearly a man for whom the future might hold significant things. He had the trust of the Vazeir if nothing else. Vyissan enjoyed his gregariousness, which leavened the dull passage of time here.

Hasen was standing at the door, and he smiled in greeting as Vyissan approached him. They talked of the weather and the season first, as they did every time they spoke, Vyissan having grown fascinated with what he could only see from his windows, and then they gradually found their way to Hasen's military career. He told Vyissan of the months of rotating scouting missions into the desert he had taken while posted near some southern city. If his geography was correct, it was not far from the imperial highway he had entered the Empire on.

"Was there much fighting out there?" Vyissan asked him.

"Not so much as you might think. I mean, they are hard enough creatures to find, and once you do they tend to just disappear before you have time to do anything. Not that we were looking for a fight either, understand. We just wanted to figure what they were about."

"And how did you do at that?"

Hasen laughed. "About as well as you might expect. Likely no better than you in the Republics."

"They are hard things to understand, under the best circumstances."

"Certainly, certainly," Hasen said. "I will tell you one thing, though. One time our quadra was caught by the Shadows in the middle of the desert. It was terrifying, I have never so feared for my life. The quadra was broken and we were scattered; only a few of us managed to survive. I'll spare you the details. Living life by the quick you almost don't even think, you just do and, at the end of it all, you wonder just what has happened.

"Three of us stayed together and survived, and we came back to the main battleground to wait and see if anyone else had fared as well. We hid ourselves as best we could and set a watch. I took the first, and what I saw will stay with me forever. It was the Shadows who returned—for their dead, I assumed. How wrong I was. The ground was littered with my friends and I saw these things come back and, on the ground where my friends lay, I watched the Shadows dance. It was a terrible, demonic thing, you cannot believe. I can only hope that my friends' souls had gone to the plains already, for their bodies were befouled. I pray that my ancestors will forgive the wrong I witnessed and did nothing to prevent."

"They are without bounds," Vyissan said.

"They do not even care for their own dead. They left them where they were. They wanted only to dance over our fallen. We didn't dare take the time to bury all our comrades, and that is something I still regret. The tolotes had them all."

"They are without bounds," Vyissan murmured again.

"Even the Craitolian heathens burn their dead."

"Indeed they do."

Later in the day, Hasen came to find him while he was writing in his journal. He formally bowed and then stood at attention.

"The Ad Eselte has requested your presence."

# 18

Uherl was waiting for him when Donier emerged from the training grounds, sweat still heavy on his robes, the afternoon sun bright in his eyes.

"You shouldn't be here," Donier said when he saw him. "What if we are seen together?"

"That is your concern, old friend," Uherl said with a grim smile as he led Donier down a side street to a run-down drinkery. The place was empty but for the proprietor. Uherl passed him some coins and he went and barred the door before retreating to a room in the back, leaving the two of them to the shadows of the main room.

Uherl gestured for him to sit and Donier did, reluctantly, trying to ignore the grime that seemed to coat the bench. The darkness made Uherl's face seem narrower than it was, the thin strands of hair that sprouted seemingly at random from his head taking on a sinister look.

"What's this all about?" Donier said, trying to keep his voice even though his heart was pounding with fear.

Uherl shook his head. "You've lost all your marrow, Donier. You're rotted all the way through."

Donier flinched at the insult but held his tongue. A brawl with this man now would solve none of his problems, tempting as it was. He needed to keep his wits about him and tread carefully.

"Do you recall at all our days in the Veil? The dreams that we shared. We dreamed of a new world, and you abandon all hope of it with the first pathetic bauble the Gver tosses your way. Has your spirit lost all its pregnancy?"

"We were children then," Donier said with a wave of his hand. "Inexperienced in the ways of the world. Some of us have grown up in the interim. Others have stayed pursuing dead causes."

Uherl smiled thinly. "Dead causes? Is that what you think? The Veil is alive and well. We shall not sit quietly any longer."

"I wish you well in your journey, then," Donier said. "But I cannot join you on it. I prefer to stay to roads less trafficked. I hope that you understand. Of course, I will say nothing of what I know of you to the Magistery, or anyone else for that matter."

"You are too kind," Uherl said, acid on his tongue. "But I am afraid we have need of you in the coming days."

Donier realized his hands were clenched into fists, and he forced himself to relax them before he said anything further. From the moment Uherl had stepped back into his life, this was what he had feared—that he would be asked to betray the Qraul and his family, all for a mad cause he no longer believed in. He said nothing as Uherl looked at him, letting the silence fester, as he imagined slitting the other's throat and leaving him to bleed out amongst the filth of this drinkery.

"You aren't going to ask what we need you to do?" Uherl said, his lips curling into a sneer as he spoke.

"It does not matter. I will not do it."

"I think you will," Uherl said. "Remember what we know."

"What you know. And what proof do you have of it?"

"Don't you recall, you were involved with the incident at the palace?" Uherl said with a grin that made Donier's blood go still. "There was a guard on duty who was involved. He ended up murdered outside the Morning grounds. You and he used to gamble there."

"Yeshar? I hardly know the man," Donier said, almost rising from his seat as he said it.

"That is not what the Chief Magister will hear, old friend. They will start an investigation. What do you think they will find?"

Donier swallowed loudly, his mouth dry. He knew nothing, other than the wild rumors that had passed through the cohort grounds, of the incident at the palace, so he did not know whether to give any credence to what Uherl was saying. Yeshar was a casual acquaintance, a man he had shared cups and bets with at the

Morning pantheon on occasion. Donier hadn't even realized the man was dead. None of that would matter, though, if the Veil had an informant who could convince the Magister, which was certainly possible. If he was placed under investigation, all his denials would sound like obfuscations to those ears, every seemingly innocuous piece of information they discovered would be made portentous, their need to provide answers to the Gver outstripping any sense. And once they started, how long until someone was discovered who could place him with the Veil all those years ago?

Uherl seemed to read his thoughts upon his face, and nodded as though they had reached an agreement. "We do not ask much of you," he said. "We cannot trust you, after all, given what you've become."

He paused a moment, considering his thoughts. "The Qraul has summoned the Gvers to Craitol. You will be named to the Qraul's guard for the journey."

"How do you plan to manage that feat?" Donier said, laughing in disbelief, the sound it echoing strangely in the empty room.

"That is not your concern, old friend. You will be appointed to his personal guard and you will go to Craitol with him. Someone there will tell you what is required of you."

"I will not kill the Gver."

"You think we would rely on you for that?" Uherl said. "Has your brain gone sodden? It will be a simple thing: the passing of a message, an absence of a few moments. Nothing that will expose you to suspicion."

His last words made Donier wince, for if they were concerned about him becoming exposed it could only mean they intended to bleed him further. He would never be free of them until he had destroyed himself and his rank so completely that he could be of no conceivable use. That was the only end he could see whichever path he chose to take. Uherl would ensure it; the years had made him bitter, Donier could tell.

Uherl stood, their audience at an end. "We will speak again once you have returned from Craitol," he said, and left the drinkery out the back door. Donier did not stir from the bench; he did not trust himself to walk anywhere yet. The whole realm seemed about to crash down around him, and he blinked his eyes rapidly, trying to steady himself.

The proprietor emerged from whatever room he had secluded

himself in, not raising an eye at the sight of Donier. He ignored him, opening the main door and retreating behind the counter ready to serve whoever entered. Donier told himself he had to leave—it would not do to be seen in here—but his body seemed unable to obey the orders of his mind. He would find a way, he told himself, to turn on Uherl and the Veil. He would not let them destroy the life he had built these last years. Jullavin would not grow into a family of no rank.

The words all sounded hollow in his mind. He forced himself to his feet and stumbled out into the daylight.

# THREE:

# ABAPOLLY

# 19

How many hours of her days, Alieren wondered, were spent performing acts devoid of substance? Like an actor upon the boards, she had her lines that she was to parrot and the steps that she was to take, but no more. Today was no different, with arrival of the first of the Gvers for the Council. Laterala, she knew, loved ceremony, but then it was all centered on him and what he was and what he represented. No matter the reality of how circumscribed his influence was, in those moments of ritual he was all powerful, the Realm itself. Whereas for Alieren, the emptiness of it all served only to remind her that she was a vessel that others filled.

She was glad to see several of the nobles of rank attending at court this morning, working hard to stifle yawns. A general course of fidgeting rippled through the crowd as they fought their restlessness. She battled the urge to sigh herself; she was on display, after all. They were all awaiting the return of the Qraul, who had gone forth to meet the Gver of Lastl at the palace gates. Most of those now assembled in the main court room had been there watching as the Gver had paid obeisance to the sovereign. No doubt there had been many snide remarks that it should have been the other way round. They had followed the Qraul and the Gver back inside, gathering in the court so that the Gver could attend, and now they awaited the two men's arrival.

This had been her daily life since her arrival at court three years ago, so sometimes it seemed an uninterrupted tedium. There was very little she could recall of that day, the first time she had been in the south, the dizzying spectacle that had engulfed her from moment she had entered the first city of the Realm had utterly overwhelmed her. She had been fifteen, terrified and lonely, about to be married to the Qraul and very likely never to see her home again.

She had sailed, along with her father and her ladies, from Lethle south and around the Azen peninsula to the mouth of the Kylep, and from there had transferred to a smaller vessel to sail upriver. Craitol was larger by far than any of the cities of the north, so her first sight of its massive walls astride the river had only furthered her sense of dislocation. The city itself and the crowds that had lined the avenues where their procession had passed dwarfed anything her imagination had been able to conjure. None of it had seemed quite real. She felt like some relic that worshipers were carrying to a temple to consecrate in the blood of an ardeh.

She remembered nothing of the ceremony that joined her to the boy Qraul. The celebration that followed seemed an endless procession of faces thrust before her own. Her face ached from smiling. She barely saw Laterala, though they were seated near one another for most of the evening. In truth, she was afraid to even look in his direction, and when her father led her to the marriage chamber, her hands were shaking. She had been so frightened that she was unable to even speak to her husband when they were left alone. It was only when she looked him in the eye and smelled the wine, heavy on his breath, that she realized he was as terrified as she was.

One of her ladies approached as the restlessness of the crowd grew louder. "Would you like me to get you something to drink, Most Gracious?"

She smiled and shook her head. The eyes of the crowd, she felt, were on her in that shared moment, and she knew it would be dissected and gossiped about through the evening celebration to follow. Her failure to produce a child was always foremost in the minds of those in the court and all her actions were taken as signs of where she had failed in her duty. It was said, she had heard, she was more interested in her ladies, and Laterala was unable to bring her to his bed. Northerners, she was told, were known to have such proclivities.

It did not matter that Laterala had his doxies; that only demonstrated her cold northern blood and failure to satisfy his needs. Not that such talk bothered her anymore. She had become inured to it and her illusions had long since been cast aside. That was as it would be. Even if she was with her third child, there would be those who would find fault with her. What she hated was the eunuch who watched her every step, to ensure that when an heir was produced it would be Laterala's child.

The Herald called out over the chatter of the crowd the approach of the Qraul. Those gathered knelt at his passing, and as he reached the top of the dais where the thrones were they prostrated themselves in full obeisance. Alieren rose and curtsied. He turned to her and lifted her to her feet, kissing her on both cheeks, and they turned to face the court. Everyone remained on their knees as the Sanadar climbed the dais and blessed them both, his hands still smelling of the ardeh he had sacrificed in the shadow of the palace gates to consecrate the entrance of the Gver.

The Gver was the next to approach the dais, announced by the Herald to the still-prostrated throng. He looked heavier than before, she thought, and worn about the eyes, which surprised her. He prostrated himself before them, paying fealty to the Qraul and the Realm. Laterala beckoned for him to rise, and the Sanadar blessed him. He embraced Laterala and kissed her on both cheeks, while she tried not to let her disgust at that dissolute, lecherous reprobate's touch register on her face.

There was more after that: an interminable procession of musicians from both courts, as well as dancers, and the insipid court poet, who had drawn up some lines for the occasion, and following that the Gver presented his gifts to the Qraul, having already presented his gifts to Craitol when he met the Herald, the Master of Ceremonies, and the Master of the Gates, just beyond the entrance to the city. Then the speeches, of course, from both the Qraul and Keleprai, praising each other, their offices, their loyalty, the Realm, the Gods, their cities, and whatever else might occur to them to give blessing to.

As she was required only to sit and observe the entire proceedings, she let her mind wander. The High Adept, she noticed, was not present. His aversion to the protocols of the state was legendary. His was the unseen hand guiding this pageantry, though, as most present would be only too aware. The stated reason for the summons of the Gvers of the Realm was the Shadow Men's incursions to the east and what might be done. Only a few, if any, in this room would be aware, as she was, that Cepedutherupt intended war as his solution—she presumed against the Shadows, though perhaps he was flexible on the matter.

She was not without her resources, though they might watch her incessantly, and she had discovered that the High Adept had contracts in place with half the mercenary companies of the north and some Enir companies as well. When she had confronted him about it, only a day before Laterala had called the Gvers to Council, he had been his typical evasive and condescending self.

"This is nothing out of the ordinary, your gracious," he said, while looking as though he wanted to ask how she had come by this information. "None of these are formal contracts; we simply have promissory notes from certain companies for soldiers, in the event of conflict. We need to know that we can have soldiers should we require. Nothing extraordinary, as I say."

All lies, for the contracts, she knew, were null following the Feast of Three, so they were signed to a purpose.

Laterala had come to her chamber that night, and afterwards they had shared a cup of wine and some fruit and talked. He was excited about something, she could tell.

She smiled at him. "What is it?"

He shrugged, smiling as well. "Nothing," he said, although he wouldn't meet her eyes.

"I see."

"I'm sworn to secrecy." He had the decency to look embarrassed. "I promised."

"I will not press it," she said. She had known in that moment that he had been given his war, the war he had desired since he had come of age. The only question had been who the High Adept would conjure as an enemy, and that had been made clear when the Council had been called.

Her throat went dry as she thought about it again, and she longed for a respite from the ceremony so that she might have something to drink, and time to think. It was left to her to stand against whatever madness the High Adept had in mind. He and the Lastl would try to lead Laterala to their poisoned well, but they were not only ones with water and they would just see where the ardeh would drink.

## 20

Byuvir Desulinyr a Kylep, Gver of that city, had arrived in the morning, enjoying the same pomp and ceremony that had been afforded Keleprai the day before. The Gver of Takyl, Duirhe, had been the first to arrive the afternoon prior to Keleprai, leaving only the Gvers of Tson, Yseltez, and, of course, Pysel still to arrive. The northern Gvers were not summoned, due to their distance and the urgency of the meeting, and while the peninsular Gvers were called upon, they would have little voice in the discussions to follow. The Council was a matter for the Great Families, and it was expected that the peninsular families would fall in line with their respective allies.

Following the ceremony, the High Adept and Keleprai left the Qraul's Palace in a veiled palanquin, surrounded by a few guards dressed as anonymous swords, through the Traitor's Gate, and were taken within the walls of an estate not far away. Cepedutherupt had requested Keleprai's presence at the meeting the day before, but had refused to say more. The clandestine nature of the proceeding irked Keleprai for some reason, though he could not say why.

Cepedutherupt had continued with his evasions as to why the Council had been summoned in their brief moments together. Laterala was more forthcoming when Keleprai had managed to get the boy alone, telling him excitedly that the High Adept had a plan to deal the Shadow Men a decisive blow. That they were somehow on the brink of a war without reason frightened him, though he had been careful to hide that from the young Qraul. What purpose could be served by this madness, he wondered, and why had Cepedutherupt excluded him from his council on this matter? That, truth be told, angered him most of all.

They entered the estate house through a servants' door, and Cepedutherupt, obviously familiar with the place, led him to a large sitting room where wine and three cups had been set out. There had been no servants on the grounds, and there were none here either. Keleprai poured them both a measure and then sprawled in a well-cushioned chair across from the High Adept.

"There is a third, I see."

"As I told you yesterday," Cepedutherupt said. "He will be along once he knows we have arrived."

"Good," Keleprai said, in a tone that suggested the opposite. He was silent for a moment. "Will you not tell me what is going on? Laterala as much as said you have an invasion planned. You cannot seriously mean to attack the Shadow Men in the desert."

"I do. There are reasons beyond the Shadows, as you shall see, though that should be more than reason enough."

They were interrupted by a polite knock to the door. They glanced at each other, as they both recalled the last time they had shared this circumstance. Cepedutherupt went and opened it, ushering in the third member of their meeting, a short and somewhat stout man who seemed vaguely familiar to Keleprai, though he could not place him.

"Attulliel a Nrai," the High Adept said by way of introduction. "You of course know the Most Illustrious Gver of Lastl."

"We have met before," the head of the Desu House said, "though that was many years ago now."

"Just after the war," Keleprai said. "You looked much younger then."

"And thinner," he said, slapping his paunch.

"That goes for us all, I think," Cepedutherupt said.

What they left unsaid was that not long after war, perhaps the next year or the year after, the Desu House had broken with the young Qraul over his marriage to a northerner. Attulliel's uncle had been the head of the House at that time and he had been outraged that, after the war he had financed and lost a son to, the Qraul would marry a northerner and not into one of the island or peninsular families. Since that time, they had sided with Apysel and their wealth, along with the Currlene House's, had ensured that Laterala's hold on the Realm stayed tenuous. That Attulliel was even present with them, especially after the decision to expand the Sea Challenge, told Keleprai that the ground was shifting even as he stood.

"Keleprai, you should know that I have been negotiating with Attulliel since before our decision to add Rakai to the Sea Challenge, though that added an urgency to the proceedings."

Cepedutherupt had filled the final cup for the merchant, who was nodding as the Adept spoke. They both sat across from Keleprai as Cepedutherupt continued.

"We had long rued, as I told Attulliel, the break between our houses that had come to pass following the war."

"As had I," the merchant declared. "Our family has always stood first by the Realm and the Qraul and that we had ceased to do so was troublesome to me."

"So, as you can see, there was a willingness to work through these issues. We have had discussions back and forth, but I think it is fair if I say that there is still much to be done. That is what today is about."

The High Adept paused to wet his mouth. "What I have today is a proposal, one I think we can easily come to an agreement on. The Qraul authorized, earlier this year, for an emissary to be sent to speak with the Emperor in Darrhyn. He went in secret, obviously, as it seemed prudent. Well, I have received word that he has been in talks with the Emperor and his advisors and they are most favorable to our plan."

"How have you received word?" Attulliel asked. Keleprai already knew the answer.

"My Disciple is the emissary. He," and here Cepedutherupt hesitated, "reached me after he had conveyed our message to the Emperor."

Keleprai shook his head against his will. They were surely far down the path of madness now. Who knew what had been promised the Desu or the Renians?

"This is what we have offered the Renians: we will supply them directly with silk. Not their merchant companies, but the Emperor himself. I believe they are eager for this to loosen the sway that the Enir Houses have in that realm. We will need someone to facilitate this and to help us control the volume of silk we send. We do not want them to exhaust all need. We also need someone who we can trust so that the secret of worms is not given over to them."

"Much as the agreement you have with the Gassin House and the trade with the Enir," Attulliel interrupted.

"Just so. And obviously we intend to offer the contract to the Desu House, provided the Qraul can be assured of its support. In this way we reestablish two ancient relationships, rectifying two grievous errors of previous Qrauls."

Attulliel leaned back in his chair, appearing to consider the offer, though Keleprai had no doubt he had already made up his mind and was simply counting the coins to come. His fortune and his grandchildren's fortunes had been assured.

"This is a great honor for both my family and my House, and I thank the Qraul for considering us for this. Of course we are willing to undertake this contract, if it is the consideration of your esteemed selves that it is for the betterment of the Realm."

"I thank you," the High Adept said. "But, as I said, we must be assured of the Desu House's support. In fact, events, which you must for the time being be left unaware about, are moving in such a way that we will need a demonstration of that loyalty and support in the near future. Perhaps very soon."

The merchant rose to his feet and retrieved the bottle of wine, replenishing all their cups. "And what would such a demonstration entail?" he said as he poured.

Cepedutherupt considered the engravings on his cup. Keleprai had already spent some time studying his. On one side there was a depiction of Melinon and Senteur coupling, while on the other Melinon and Ulternon shared an intimate embrace. Around the rim of the cup and its base, their human children engaged in various acts of congress following their glorious example.

The High Adept did not speak until the merchant had returned to his seat. "If the Apysel should come to you for funds at any time this season we would ask that you would deny them."

"You are asking a great deal," Attulliel replied with a frown. "You would have me end one feud only to begin another. I had thought that with our new understanding we might work toward bringing all the Great Families and all the nobles of rank together. In these troublesome times, which after all is why you are gathering here now, would this not be a wiser choice?"

"I understand that it is a great condition, but it is one that we must place. With the silk agreement, no matter the details of the agreement, which we will need to work out, you stand to gain far more than you will lose."

The merchant shifted uncomfortably in his seat. Cepedutherupt smiled benevolently at him, as though he had not just asked to place a knife at his throat.

Keleprai wondered if the High Adept had miscalculated here, for the risk was now just as great as the reward for the Desu, particularly for Attulliel. Pervelte a Pysel was justly legendary for his desire to exact vengeance on those who crossed him. Just this past winter, he had torn the genitals from a noble of the fourth rank, whom he believed had betrayed the Apysel for revealing a secret to a dancer of the Midday from Takyl. He had scorched the man's nose from his face as well, for it was well known that the soul of honesty and trust resided in the nose. He had concluded by having the man wrecked on the wheel in public, a shocking punishment for someone of rank.

Just as he was thinking this through, Keleprai realized how the Adept intended to seal the new alliance. He had wondered why he had been asked to attend today when he had not been privy to any of the earlier negotiations, and now he knew. The knowledge sparked his bitterness again at not being included in the Cepedutherupt's council, especially when it was plain now that much would depend on his acceding to the High Adept's wishes. Cepedutherupt would call it a sign of his trust and their shared understanding of the Realm, but to Keleprai it signaled that he was no more than Laterala—a puppet to be given voice to whenever Cepedutherupt had need of him.

"It is not the loss of business that concerns me," Attulliel said. "As you say, we shall not want for money, and business has a way of returning, regardless of changing winds. No, if I am to cross the Apysel, I need to know that I will not simply be left to suffer whatever depravations they determine to visit upon my house."

"We cannot give you any greater protection than you already likely employ. The Apysel are not demons or fiends capable of sifting through the walls of your estates and striking you as you sleep."

"I do not worry for myself. The dangers that all of us here face do not change from day to day, no matter the circumstance of the Realm. My concern is for those associated with me, whom I will place in grave danger should I do this. You would not ask me if you didn't believe that the Apysel will approach our House for funds this season. I will not be able to agree to this, no matter how much we stand to gain, unless I have some…assurance that I will not be paying for this in blood for the next decade."

Cepedutherupt put a hand to his chin, as though he were pondering this possibility for the first time. He glanced over at Keleprai and their eyes met for a moment, an understanding shared.

"I believe that we might be able to provide such assurance as you seek," Cepedutherupt said, and turned to Keleprai, who smiled in turn, quelling the bile that threatened to rise to his tongue. What if he refused him this? It was no use, the High Adept would have his alliance with the Desu somehow, just as he would have his alliance with the Renians, just as surely as they would go to war in the desert before the season was out. All his refusal would achieve was the casting out of the Alastl from the Qraul's embrace.

"I agree with the illustrious Adept," he said, wondering if his distaste for the words had shown. "It is something that should have been done long ago by one of the Great Families, and here is an opportunity now for us to right another ancient wrong.

"If I am remembering correctly, your sister is married to the Gver of Nrai, Assuard Festunyr, and they were blessed, twelve years ago, with the birth of a daughter, Cerries. As I'm sure you know, my wife and I were blessed with a son, who will be fourteen come the fall. If I am not mistaken, neither has been promised to anyone as yet."

"This is true," Attulliel said, running his tongue along his upper lip as he contemplated this.

"And it is also true," Cepedutherupt said, "that the Anrai have long sought and long been denied a marriage within the Great Families, for reasons long past the need for dwelling on."

Keleprai nodded, draining his cup, his mouth dry. "You spoke of bringing the families and the nobles together. Well, what would do more than righting that long omission by allowing the Mgetir nobility to enter the greater family of the Realm?"

"You would truly give your son to the Anrai," Attulliel said, with an eyebrow raised as though he suspected some ruse.

"I would. It makes sense for the Alastl, for the Anrai, the Desu, and the Realm, beyond simply the momentary needs and politics of this season."

"I would of course have to discuss this with Nes Assuard."

"Naturally," Keleprai said, and both he and Cepedutherupt smiled. Assuard was Attulliel's man; it was the Desu House that truly ruled in Nrai. *And I*, Keleprai thought, *am the High Adept's man truly.*

"But I do not foresee any problems there."

"So, we have assurance as to the other?" Cepedutherupt asked.

Attulliel nodded, and they all stood and clasped arms to seal the agreement. The merchant stepped away from them and walked over to a cabinet behind the table where the wine had been set out. He unlocked it with a key he drew from his robes and took a bottle of auth from it, an amber liquor from the Mgetir Isle, and three sipping glasses. He poured a finger for each of them and they all raised their glasses and downed it in a gulp.

They discussed the agreement after the drink, settling on some of the details and promising to meet again in a few days after the Council was complete. When that was done, Attulliel excused himself, saying he needed to send word to his factors and Nes Assuard. The High Adept led Keleprai back out the way they had come, the palanquin lowered and awaiting them, and they began their journey back to the palace.

They were silent for a time, the unseen chatter of the street drifting to them as they went along. Cepedutherupt was the first to speak.

"So you see, we do not need to worry about the Realm. The Realm will be unified. The Apysel will not dare stand against us if they do not have the gold, and today we have assured they will not."

Keleprai was a long time in replying. "I see the wisdom in this…obviously. You bring the Rakai nobility and merchants onside by giving them the Challenge, and you bring the Nrai in with this."

"The rest of the peninsulars will no doubt fall in line as well, if they believe—and why wouldn't they—that we are willing to give them more than simple tokens."

Keleprai nodded. "Clearly. The Apysel is not the ball to bet on now. I'm shocked that you were able to pull the Desu from them."

Cepedutherupt smiled. "It would not have happened without the Renians."

"What else have they agreed to, I wonder."

"Everything we proposed."

"So they are willing to attack the Shadows?" Keleprai shook his head. "Madness in all realms. I can't believe this. You of all people should know the consequences of what you propose. And now you've gotten it into that boy's head as well."

"I do know the consequences of what I propose. I also know the consequences of inaction, which nearly was the undoing of the Realm before. And make no mistake, they pose the same threat as Kercubegahedd. The Shadows have the knowledge of the engines now. Do you think that they will rest easy in the desert now that they have it?"

It seemed pointless to argue with the High Adept now, when he had given up his coin for stamping, like any academy trull, without so much as a word in dispute. "So you would have us run around the wastelands so that the Council might destroy the machines."

"No. If they were scattered there would be no hope. My fear is that soon they will be."

The palanquin came to an abrupt halt, though they had yet to pass through the gates to the palace. Cepedutherupt went silent and Keleprai swallowed loudly. He hated being enclosed in the carriage, unable to see. There was a rap at the side of palanquin from one of the guards with them.

"My apologies, Most Gracious, but there is a disturbance ahead."

"What sort of disturbance?" Cepedutherupt demanded.

"That is difficult to say." There was a long pause. "There is a cloister on fire ahead and some fighting in the street."

Keleprai strained to hear and could just discern the shouts and cries, though it was hard to say that it was anything more than just the life of the street.

Cepedutherupt thought a moment. "Send one of your men to the local Magisterium. We will continue on to the palace by another route."

"Yes, Most Gracious," the guard said, and shouted instructions to one of his men. With another order, they began to move again. After a moment, the High Adept called to the guard again.

"What cloister was it that was burning?"

"I'm not certain, Most Gracious," was the unseen reply. "We are on Ressel, near the Alafheri markets."

Cepedutherupt thanked him and then turned to Keleprai. "It is the Hasierren. A Lasisen cloister. I can tell you, my greatest concern at the moment is the boy's mother and her heresy."

As the palanquin was carried along its new route, the wind shifted and the smell of the fire reached them. Keleprai shivered at it, unable to stifle the sense of terror that immediately clenched his veins. He had been eleven or twelve when Lastl had been struck by the Great Fire and a quarter of the city had burned. He had never forgotten watching from the walls of the palace as the conflagration spread, smoke covering over the whole sky, and then he and his nursemaid, and others of their household, had been taken away in palanquins in the dead of night outside the city to the family's country estate, where he had spent a week before returning to the still-smoking remains of the city.

It took a moment for him to quiet his fear, before his thoughts ventured back to Dalenna. Dreams of her still preoccupied some of his nights, the ones where he managed sleep at all. He wondered if this was Ulternon, who guided all dreams, trying to speak to him, something of import. He had thought them nothing more than lustful memory, pinings for his lost youth. All very pathetic at best, the beginnings of senility at worst. But maybe there was something more to it. Only the smiling of the Gods could explain all that was happening here.

Cepedutherupt, as if reading his thoughts, said, "She will not speak to me, but maybe she will with you. You did grow up together, after a fashion."

"Yes, we did," Keleprai said. "Indeed we did."

# 21

The Ad Eselte was working in one of the Imperial Libraries, the librarians having been temporarily banished. In the seven days he had been gone from Darrhyn, two new texts had arrived and he wanted to view one in particular, a discourse on mazes and labyrinths and the mathematical principles behind them. It was the work of the scholar Messillah, written perhaps three hundred years before and long thought lost. One of his agents had discovered a copy in a sanctuary in Tyresih and had smuggled it back into the Empire. It was a recent copy, judging by its fine shape, the spine still strong and the pages all whole in spite of the arduous journey it had undergone.

He had long held a fascination with the principles of mazes and their history, in no small part because beneath the Imperial Palace there lay a maze of tunnels that stretched, in ever-expanding circles, beyond the walls of the palace proper. Most called it a labyrinth, though the Ad Eselte knew that was not correct. Most architects, following Messillah, made a distinction between a maze, which was meant to puzzle and entrap whoever was in it, and a labyrinth, where there was only one through path and the goal was not confusion, but rather an ordered pattern. What lay below was intended to obfuscate and obstruct all but those who had its key, and there were multiple ways through the rooms and halls, depending on where one sought to go.

He had used the tunnels to leave Darrhyn, emerging outside the city walls just a short walk to a little-used dock that was manned at all times by some of his most trusted guard. From there he had gone, not to his paradise, as Ibrazol had told those who had to be told, but north and inland to Asieren, Ibrazol's hunting paradise. There, with Usen and a few trusted others from his court, he had spent five long days, the heat and insects insufferable, amidst the spare furnishings of his Vazeir's lodge.

Usen coughed politely, interrupting his thoughts, and he glanced up. His castulan frowned and glanced back over his shoulder.

"Send him in," the Ad Eselte said. "Now is as good a time as any."

"Yes, Most Immortal," Usen said, and walked back to the library doors to tell the guard to let Ibrazol in.

Watching his Vazeir approach, the Ad Eselte was struck again by how little they knew of the workings of this plain, no matter what principles of mazes and labyrinths they might elaborate. Only their ancestors, granted the perspective of the plains above, could provide true guidance and illumination. He was thinking this because Ibrazol, when faced with the sudden appearance of an Enir claiming to be an emissary of the Qraul of Craitol, had not even given a thought that the man might be telling the truth, for the truth was far too outlandish to be believed.

Given that he had been only days away from striking at the conspirators who sought the overthrow of the Empire, and given that he had no idea how close they were to enacting whatever plans they had in mind, Ibrazol had assumed that the Enir who had asked for an imperial audience was involved in the plot in some way. This seemed especially prudent since the man he had arranged to meet in the palace was an administrator who had been involved in the murder of their Luessan agent and then been murdered himself. Fearing that their plans were already in motion, he had come to the Ad Eselte and urged him to flee the city until he had crushed the insurrection.

What the poor man must have been thinking, imprisoned in the Vazeir's Palace? By ancestors' grace, Ibrazol had done nothing to him. He was a judicious man, though. And when the guard to which he had set the task of befriending the Enir reported back that the man seemed to know little of the Empire, well, it was reasonable to assume that he might be telling the truth. A safer conclusion to draw with the conspirators arrested and dead, and none of them revealing any plans involving a fake emissary from Craitol.

When the Ad Eselte had returned, the bodies of the traitors still fresh on the walls, Ibrazol had shown him the emissary's letter of introduction with the seal of the Qraul. No emperor had set eyes on that seal in thirty years or more, and so there had been a search through the archives for some earlier missive. It had been days before one of the archivists emerged with a letter, the ink on it gone illegible but the seal still clear where it had been branded atop the paper.

They had spoken with the man the day before, late in the afternoon, and the Ad Eselte had asked for the night to think on what had been said before they discussed it again. And now here was Ibrazol, impatient as always, the light of the day still fresh upon the land.

"I have not come to any decision," he said, after the Vazeir had bowed. He gestured for Ibrazol to sit. "Do you believe what the man says? Is he who he says he is?"

Ibrazol nodded. "I do, Most Gracious. None of the trails from the conspirators led to him. And I find it difficult to believe that they would have been able to find the seal to replicate it. How many days did it take your archivists?"

"Three," the Ad Eselte said. "No, I agree. He is who he says is. The question, it seems, is do we believe what he has to say?"

"I don't see any reason why not, Most Beneficent. There is risk for us if we go ahead with their plan. And much to gain. They have already chanced much in sending this man here, if he is what he says he is. And why would he lie? It is too easily exposed."

The Ad Eselte considered this, placing his palms together in invocation. "The lie would be too great a risk if discovered. I am not certain about the risk in going through with their invasion, though. We do not know why they are considering this and what they hope to gain. I would assume they have other irons in the fire."

"As would we, Most Immortal. As would we. The risk and the gain are the same for both, I should think. And the gift he offers in exchange for our joining them is great. It would, I think, more than make up for whatever we might lose in such a battle."

"The Craitolian silk? Yes, that is what concerns me most, actually." The Ad Eselte paused as he considered his words, running his hand along the open page of the text before him. "It concerns me precisely because the offer is so great. I would have expected a payment to be offered for our support, but this is well beyond that. You are correct—in the long term we will be stronger no matter the outcome of this particular battle. I cannot fathom why they would want that."

"The enemy of mine."

"Perhaps. But if they have the wealth that they appear to, and that we certainly have long surmised, then how long will the Shadows be who they are concerned with? We, or the Republics, that is in the long run, who must stand opposed to their ambitions, whatever they may be."

The Vazeir twitched in his seat and the Ad Eselte resisted a smile. He knew the man well enough to know whenever he was getting restless. Talk always did so, especially debate.

"Why should we do this?" he asked.

Ibrazol considered the question. "The silk trade, Most Beneficent. It will fill our coffers at the expense of the Republics. We would strengthen ourselves with regard to the Three Kingdoms as well.

"If we are successful in the desert—no sure thing, granted, but if we were—we would stabilize our western border. With the threat there diminished, we can shift our focus to the east and our Luessan problem, which recent events have shown is a significant one. Internally, as well, I think this is good. Remember Walleen. When the Nohritai are disaffected, best to offer them some chance to make their names."

The Ad Eselte nodded. "These are strong arguments. My first concern is the silk trade. Why is the offer so great, when much less would likely suffice? We face the same problems with the Shadow Men they do."

"Perhaps, Most Illustrious, they do not know that. The emissary seems to know little of us."

"Perhaps. My second concern is the war itself. Nothing in the desert is sure, no matter the force we take there. There is no guarantee that they will return with any sort of strength. That would weaken us greatly in the near term. Our position against the Luessans in the north is still so weak."

Ibrazol did not reply, his hand tapping out a silent rhythm on the table.

"You believe we should do this?"

"I do, Most Beneficent."

"If we go to war, your son would be elevated."

"The Ad Ezern have always been willing to sacrifice whatever is needed for the Empire, Most Illustrious."

The Ad Eselte nodded. "So you have. And your loss does not go unnoticed, nor will it be forgotten."

The Vazeir was silent again. The Emperor looked at him for a moment longer and said, "I would think on this."

Ibrazol nodded and rose to his feet. He took his leave and walked out of the doors to library. Usen was inside before the door had a chance to shut completely, and the Ad Eselte waved him back, returning to the volume open before him.

## 22

Kigarle Vistuvyr was unsure if he was surrounded by mysterious, and potentially malignant, goings on here in the Palace of the Qraul, or if it was just his imagination gone mad, fed by his own worry and the whispers that had haunted him since they had left Lastl for the capital. Threats seemed to loom from every corner, each gathering of courtiers in the narrow corridors potentially part a plot to murder the Gver, each lone figure standing, apparently without purpose, an assassin in disguise. Such thoughts could unhinge a man, he well knew, but he could not stop himself from thinking them. Better that than to worry on his guilt in the matter, which had kept him from sleep for days.

The first whispers had come as the Gver prepared to leave Lastl, the Council having been summoned. Keleprai, as he always did, appointed Kigarle to see to his retinue for the trip. A man, craggy-faced and with stringy hair, a scarecrow come to life, had found him late one evening in a drinkery, well into his cups, and had whispered what he knew of Kigarle and what he expected him to do for his silence. Kigarle had said nothing, staying to drink until the memory was nearly obliterated, seeming more a dream than reality.

He might have been able to convince himself that it had been but a dream if not for the letter delivered to him at his estate the next day. It had been unsigned, but the seal was of the leaf of a rasgon, a tree found only in the desert. Enir, whether they were from the Republics or native to Craitol, often adopted it as an emblem for their businesses or badges. The contents of the letter were immaterial; the leaf was enough to tell Kigarle that the night before had not been a dream but was part of an ongoing nightmare, one that continued to hound his days even in the first city of the Realm.

It did not help that the man who he had brought to Craitol at the request of unnamed interloper appeared as agitated and out of sorts as Kigarle felt. Donier a Fieled was his name, a noble of the third rank. They had met before at various official occasions, though Kigarle did not remember him beyond his name. The kehel of his cohort Ludenn, a man Kigarle trusted, had spoken highly of him, telling him that Donier would lead a cohort some day. All in all, the sort of man who might have been selected to join the Gver's retinue anyway under normal circumstances, a reward for his service. But these were not normal days—all was being torn asunder, or so it seemed to Kigarle.

This day in particular had been trying. Keleprai had disappeared following Gver Byuvir's arrival at court, along with the High Adept, an absence which had been noted by everyone, only serving to increase the tensions among the various retinues now gathered in the palace. It would only get worse, especially once the Apysel arrived and began their usual scheming. Keleprai had been in a furious mood following his return and had spent the evening getting riotously drunk and trying his luck with half the ladies of the court, further enraging the other nobles gathered there.

Kigarle had saved the situation as best he could by securing the services of one of the Evening dancers performing at court, and had sent the Gver on his way. Now, restless and unable to find sleep, and his head beginning to ache from the wine he had drunk himself, he found himself wandering the corridors of the Lastl quarters in the First Palace, assuring himself that everything was fine. Keleprai was still with the dancer, he assumed, and the guards he had posted outside his doors were still on duty, though the sounding the of hour would signal the end of their watch. Otherwise the halls were quiet, everyone having retreated to their beds.

Near the Gver's quarters there was a balcony overlooking one of the many palace gardens, and Kigarle headed there after he was done with his rounds to take some air. As he stepped out, his eyes going to the stars, an invocation to Senteur upon his lips, he realized he was not alone. Donier was leaning against the balcony railing, peering down into the shadows of the garden. The noble glanced up at Kigarle's entrance, his morose expression transformed by unease which he could not disguise.

"Can't sleep, Nes Donier?" Kigarle said, forcing a smile to his lips. The other shook his head, not meeting his gaze. They were both bathed by the dim glow of the lanterns that illuminated the corridor behind them, granting them both a sinister aspect.

"Nor can I," Kigarle added when the other did not speak. "The days will only grow more difficult, I fear."

Donier nodded, not taking his eyes from the darkness below. Kigarle watched him a moment, wondering what he was thinking. It was obvious he wanted to be left alone, and to be honest Kigarle wanted the same, but he could not resist taking this opportunity to find out what he could of the man and why he was here. He had done what the letter asked him, but that did not mean he had to sit idly by now.

"It is a great honor for you to be appointed to the Gver's retinue. Your kehel speaks most highly of you."

Donier turned to him, sensing that he would not escape without a conversation. "I never dreamed it possible. The Gods have blessed me."

"We shall see about that," Kigarle said. "If things go wrong, you will be blamed."

Donier looked at him, fear seeping into his expression. Kigarle laughed, waving a hand at him. "You are the new man here," he said, "when people are looking to apportion blame they always look to the new man."

"We are in the Qraul's Palace, though," Donier said. "Under flag of truce. What do you think could happen?"

Kigarle shook his head. "You do not know the Apysel. Pervelte is not constrained by such niceties, I can assure you. And he is not the only one."

Donier nodded sadly, returning his gaze to the darkness. Kigarle turned his attention there as well, thinking the man appeared as concerned at what might befall them as he did, as if Donier truly did believe the blame would fall upon him no matter what. A strange man, he thought, to be given such a task by the Veil. He was nothing at all like the others Kigarle had had the ill fortune of meeting.

"I wonder what this is all about. What does the Qraul want with this?"

"The High Adept, you mean," Kigarle said with a smile. "Keleprai has told me nothing, but they will have something in mind and the Apysel and others will be looking to thwart it. These are the games we always play. The Gods laugh at us."

The exhaustion that had been on the edge of his being all night suddenly seized him whole as he stood there, his own words signaling the futility of what he was trying to do here. Donier would not tell him anything. For all he knew the Veil had a hold on him as well. All he could do now was be vigilant. He had made his choices and would have to live with them somehow should anything go foul.

"They do," Donier said, and pushed himself from the ledge, heading past Kigarle into the palace, giving a nod as he went past. Kigarle could read nothing from his expression, though he felt for some reason it had been significant.

*I am going mad*, he thought, and studied his own hands, bathed in shadows and murk. Who could blame him, though—it was his son, after all.

The day Adrenah had come to Kigarle, tears staining his eyes, begging him to recognize him so that he would be a man of rank and could escape punishment for his crimes, was rarely far from his thoughts. It could emerge from the dark tangle of his emotions to lance his heart at any moment, no matter what he was doing. The boy was his, he had always acknowledged that, but his mother was an Enir and a trull and so he could never recognize him. It was impossible, as he had explained—out of the question. He would risk his own rank and the inheritance of his sons to do so.

He had done more than many others would have for the boy. Not only had he acknowledged him, when he first heard from the trull, a girl named Nasiff, that she was with child, he had set her up in a home and paid her an allowance. She remained his mistress, the one love of his life, and the three other children she had given him had brought him nothing but joy. Adrenah had always been ill-starred, though, getting into trouble from the moment he could walk, and when he had come of age he started to associate himself with men of ill repute.

Kigarle had extricated him from a few predicaments, but they seemed only to spur the boy into further outrages, as if to mock his father's propriety. The last had proven too much even for Kigarle to save him, a murder of some criminal in a drunken fight, for which a vendetta had been sworn against Adrenah. The boy had come to his father, seeking the protection of rank, and when that had been denied him he had gone to the Veil. They had promised him protection in exchange for payment, which only Kigarle could provide. His inclusion of Donier in the retinue was but the first installment, he knew—the Veil would bleed him so long as Adrenah was alive. And he had to, he told himself; he could not refuse the boy, and especially not his mother. He was her first child, her favorite. Kigarle well understood the price and he was willing to pay it.

As he continued to stare into the darkness, he realized there was nothing else for it but to try again to sleep, though he knew in his bones sleep would not come. His thoughts would only grow bleaker staying here, and at least he had a bottle of wine in his room to pass the time. Morning would come soon enough.

# 23

Ten days had passed since the clamorous evening of raids and arrests. In its immediate aftermath, a calm had settled over Darrhyn, as though with the cessation of the raids and the threat of violence from the Imperial Guard, people were allowed a great exhalation. It was fleeting sensation, for it had been a bizarre summer, marred by killings, insurrections thwarted, and Shadow Men breaching the unbreachable walls of the imperial city, and that did not cease following the execution of the conspirators. The anxiety that had preyed on so many in the weeks and months before returned to seize them in full again. Chroniclers in later years would always take care to note these and other events as proof that these were indeed the strangest of times, when it seemed as though the very foundations of Renian society might be crumbling at their feet, shaken by some unseen tremor their ancestors only knew of.

The latest violations to the established order were perhaps the most disturbing and perverse of all: the desecration of some sanctuaries and tombs by agents unknown. People sought to explain it by saying it was supporters of the Ad Eselte exacting revenge on the conspirators' families by vandalizing their holy places, but it soon became clear that there was no pattern to the defilement. Raids of mausoleums were not unknown, which was why the most important Nohritai families had theirs within the walls of their estates, but this was a different thing again. Tombs were broken into, but few valuables were taken. Instead, relics were shattered, the resting places of ancestors disturbed, and there was urine and feces left everywhere. Those families that could afford it put guards around their mausoleums, and some banded together to keep watch over the cemeteries, but it did not seem to matter—a few tombs were struck each night.

Many said it had to be the Shadows committing these acts, for no Renian could possibly turn to such foul ends. That no one had seen the desecrators lent credence to this theory, and in its way it was more reassuring to think that there were Shadow Men moving unseen amongst them than to contemplate the alternative. There began to be talk of the need to regain their knowledge of the alkemyc arts in order to expose these false men.

It was the only thing anyone could speak of, and Masiph had grown tired of it. There had been desecrations before, and there would no doubt be further and more unspeakable ones to follow. Such was existence on this plain, and had been for all recorded time. The Empire, once so great, was now fallen, and the world was smaller and less majestic with each passing year.

He could be forgiven not caring, for he had somehow, in spite of his own foolishness, escaped retribution for his part in the conspiracy. The ecstasy at being alive that he had expected in some way to seize him after he had recovered from his injuries at the hand of the Shadow had at last taken hold of him and had not let go in the four days since he had gone looking at the dead.

He had taken to walking the streets, any and all, even in the depths of night, without any care or concern for his own person. Ancestors would provide. Sometimes he dressed in his Craitolian silks and others in common robes, wandering from drinking room to drinking room, all manner of establishments, from the dregs to the most exclusive. It was all to no real end, other than that he could. He talked without a care, taunting whomever he took exception to, surprising himself with his lacerating tongue. As a result, he found himself in a few brawls, the sort of melees that drew in men on all sides and ended only with bruises, blood, and humiliation.

Only once did he find himself in a duel, and even that was only because of his own stupidity. He had stumbled into the alley behind the drinkery he found himself in to piss, when a man he had insulted earlier set upon him with a knife. Masiph had been lucky that it had been a clear night, otherwise he would never have seen the man as he approached. As it was, he had to fight with his robes in a tangle, his penis still exposed, though shrinking rapidly. He was fortunate the man was far drunker than he, for he was able to knock him from his feet and flee without anything more coming of it.

Every place he went to, he made sure to ask if anyone knew of a courtesan who was also an assassin. No one, even when he described what she looked like, had heard anything of her. It was, he supposed, not surprising that she was not well known in the drinkeries of the city. She could not very well be an effective killer if half the capital recognized her. He racked his mind, trying to think of where and how he might best look for her, hindered, he knew, by the fact that he did not know—nor did he want to—how one went about hiring an assassin.

After four days of asking, he had a sense that he would likely never find her. There was a very good chance she did not even live in Darrhyn, though all the world did. He could not even say why exactly he was looking for her; there were women as beautiful in any number of academies across the city. He was possessed with the image of her casually sitting, one leg crossed artfully over the other, her victim splayed on the bed behind her. The thought of it excited him for reasons he did not even want to think about fully.

Still and all, life was good for Masiph following the end of the conspiracy. The agonizing he had drawn himself through those past weeks had evaporated, and all that lay before him were empty hours in search of something to pass the days. For the time being, that was all he desired. Likely that was a good thing, for he still thought his father suspected him of some malfeasance, meaning his chances at an elevation and a good marriage were past. And what of it, if it were so? Best to resign himself to that eventuality now than continue to live in the shadows of its dread.

The morning of the fifth day since he had emerged from his rooms and returned to the world, he set out across the city, wandering aimlessly. He stopped in at public chewing room and passed an hour in talk with the Nohritai and merchants there. Two more mausoleums had been struck, one at the Nohritai cemetery in Isinan, another in a merchant cemetery across the city. They were far enough apart that it meant there had to be more than one group perpetrating these acts. Masiph listened to various theories put forth, not giving the matter much thought himself, before heading back into the streets, letting all the talk wash away.

He had been walking for about half an hour when he began to sense that he was being followed. It stayed with him for the rest of the day as he wandered, and though he stopped several times, and doubled back on his trail, as Nazeed had taught him, he was unable to reveal any perpetrator or shake the feeling, even once he returned to Isinan and the Ad Ezern estate.

# 24

Quesin announced himself to her formally, bowing as he stepped into her outer bedchamber, something he almost never did, so Nyzren knew that her father had come to see her. He always insisted on such ceremony. She decided to receive him in one of her sitting rooms. Not here. This was hers.

She had one of her ladies fetch a bottle of wine and some fruit—if they were going to be formal—and then told Quesin to send Osiphan in.

"Daughter," he called her as he came into the room, clasping her hands in his and kissing her forehead.

"Father," she said, and led him across the room to the divans, where they sat, the wine and fruit between them. Quesin appeared on cue with two glasses, and with a practiced flourish he opened the bottle and poured out a measure for the two of them before retreating from the room.

She waited for him to speak first. She knew why he was here, of course. He took one of the glasses and had a sip and then raised it to her in thanks. She took her glass in hand but did not drink yet.

At last Osiphan spoke. "Tomorrow we are to honor Hissell, as you know. I have spoken to the Corenedor of the Guard"—and here the words were hard for him—"and he has granted permission for us to do so."

There was a long pause and she took a drink of wine, more for something to do than anything else. She tried to think of something to say, but couldn't find anything she thought suitable.

"I would very much appreciate your presence at the ceremony tomorrow."

"Of course I will go," Nyzrella said.

He let out a small sigh and took a long drink of his wine. He wasn't sure of her intentions, she thought, surprised. She had never known him to be uncertain about anything. It had never crossed her mind not to attend; she had in fact been looking forward to it, hoping that both her parents would emerge from their seclusion for the ceremony. That the Guard might not allow the ceremony to go forward stunned her. It was their tombs, after all, their ancestors. Even the Imperial Guard would not dare defy a Nohritai's ancestors—at least, she didn't imagine they would.

"Your mother," he said, choosing his words carefully still, "has sent word that she will not be joining us. She may never forgive me."

No, she will not, Nyzrella thought, but did not say. What was there to say? Osiphan looked as if he had not slept in the past two days. Likely he had not. She thought of his words that night in the library: *Nobody knows what the next days will hold.* Perhaps things had not gone as he had hoped.

Osiphan set his glass aside, appearing unsure of what to say next, and Nyzren felt compelled to take his hands in hers. He flinched at her touch, his face going red, and nodded his thanks, at last summoning the words he wished to say.

"Would you be willing to go to her, to help her see reason on this matter? She will not let me enter her quarters. I cannot speak to her."

The admission was a difficult one, she could see, giving voice to the fact that he was no longer master of this house and its inhabitants. He had truly lost everything, she realized, and the thought struck fear in her. There was no telling what next days would bring, but none of it would be good, she suspected.

"Of course, father," she said, squeezing his hands.

"Thank you, Nyzren," he said, emotion high in his voice, which surprised her again.

"I don't know if she will hear my words either," she said. Osiphan shrugged, a gesture that suggested he had no hope in the matter but what else was there to be done and Nyzren nodded in turn. Her father finished his wine and took his leave, and she was left to wonder what was happening. Was everything about to tumble even further into the abyss?

She went to see her mother later that afternoon, the shadows beginning to lengthen toward dusk as she made her way along the hallway that connected their rooms in the woman's quarters of the Ad Reteln estate. They were on the second floor of the estate, with the eunuchs and ladies living below, while her grandmother, much to Usyre's chagrin, had the rooms on the third floor to herself. Her mother often talked bitterly of how the house would never be hers, for that woman would outlive them all. Now it seemed that prediction had come true in a sense, for the estate would never be theirs again.

Nyzren wondered what the old woman thought of the events of the past days, deciding that, in all likelihood, she remained unaware. She rarely left her rooms anymore, spending most of her hours in bed, her health in a delicate state. Osiphan would have sworn her eunuchs and ladies to keep the truth from her at a cost of their lives. And they would have, for they all despised Usyre and wanted to ensure that they could remain free of her rule for as many days as their ancestors would allow.

She was ushered through the outer rooms of her mother's quarters to the inner chamber, where one of her ladies and the eunuch Ghat, a beautiful and insolent young thing, idled. Usyre was apparently still in bed, and the lady went within to announce Nyzren to her while Ghat made himself busy avoiding her gaze. The girl returned a moment later to say that Usyre would be seeing no one that day.

"She will see me," Nyzren said, with what she hoped was an imperious tone, and marched past the startled girl into her mother's bedchamber.

She came to a stop almost immediately after passing through the threshold, horror at the sight of her mother bringing her to a stunned halt. Usyre, who had always been so proper, each strand of hair, each robe and jewel carefully placed just so, lay in bed still in her nightdress, which by the look of it she had been wearing for some time, her hair falling in messy tangles around her head. She was staring distantly up at the canopy of her bed, a dreamy look in her eyes, seemingly not having realized that Nyzrella had entered the room.

Nyzren took a step toward her mother, halting again, unsure of what exactly to do or say. She had never seen her mother like this. It was nothing like what she had expected. There were no tears; she was not raging against Osiphan as Nyzren had so often heard her. This, whatever it was, was far, far worse.

Behind her, Ghat cleared his throat loudly, interrupting her thoughts. When she turned to face the eunuch, he said, "Husem Usyre does not wish to see anyone, Husem. You should leave."

"You are telling me where I can go in my own home?" Nyzrella said. "You? Mind your place."

The eunuch flinched at her words but stood his ground. All the emotion, her sadness at the world taken from her and her fear at what was to come, came boiling forth in a fury she could not contain. She struck Ghat, her fingers scratching his face, leaving a red mark on his cheek. His own shade deepened as emotion seized him, and for a moment Nyzren thought he would return her blow with one of his own. He did not and she struck him again, hard enough to turn his head.

"Get out," she said. "Get out. You are not to enter this room while I am here and you are not to speak to me again."

The eunuch pursed his lips, fury marring his beautiful features, but he turned and left the room without another word. Nyzren shut the door behind him and went to her mother's side, touching her forehead and finding no fever. Usyre still seemed unaware of her presence, and Nyzren saw that her eyes were unfocused, still staring off into some imagined distance even when she thrust her face directly into her mother's line of vision.

"What have you done, mother?" she said, her voice trembling with emotion. She looked at her hands and saw that they were shaking as well, the aftermath of her confrontation with Ghat seizing her. Under normal circumstances her mother would be furious with her for defying her wishes and ordering her servants about as she had, and part of her still feared that she would suffer some consequence for what she had done. Though looking at Usyre as she lay there, she knew none would be forthcoming.

"Mother," she said gently, taking her clammy hand in her own. "Mother, tell me what has happened. You must speak to me."

Usyre's eyes fluttered and at last settled upon Nyzren's face, and she frowned and turned away, shaking her head.

"Look at me, mother," Nyzren said. "You have to look at me."

Usyre withdrew her hand from her daughter's grasp, turning

and burying her face in her pillow. "I want to see Ghat," she said, pronouncing each word slowly as though she were unsure of their meaning.

"He isn't here," Nyzren said. "I'm here, mother. You can talk to me."

"No, you are his daughter."

Nyzren felt her air go from her chest and she had to force herself to breathe. "I am your daughter too," she said, putting a hand on her mother's shoulder.

Usyre flinched at her touch, as though she had been scalded. "No, you are his daughter. You have always been his. There is nothing of mine left."

Nyzren tried to find words to speak, but they would not come. She left her mother to her reverie, retreating from the room to the outer chamber, where both the lady and Ghat awaited her. As soon as she had closed the door behind her, Ghat moved to stand in front of it, glaring at her possessively.

She turned to the lady and said, pointing at the eunuch, "He is not to see my mother. No one is without my permission."

"I do not serve you," Ghat said, his hands curling into fists.

"I told you you were not to speak to me," Nyzren said. "Leave this room immediately. Tequihan will tell you what is required of you now."

She turned to the lady, not even bothering to see if Ghat left, though she could hear his steps out of the room and feel his gaze upon her back. She said to the girl, who stood openmouthed, "Will you do as I say?"

The girl quailed under her gaze and said, "Yes, Husem."

"Good," Nyzren said. "Mind the door and let no one in but myself or Tequihan."

Next she went to find the castulan of the woman's quarters and discovered him on the way to her own quarters.

"Husem, what is wrong? What has happened?" he said, a perplexed look upon his face.

"Ghat is not to see my mother anymore."

Tequihan raised a judicious eyebrow. "Very well, Husem," he said. "She will not be pleased."

"She is no longer in her right mind. She is not fit to run these quarters and neither is my grandmother, so it would seem those duties must now fall to me. Will you serve me as you did my mother?"

"I will, Most Beautiful Husem," he said with a smile. "I will indeed."

## 25

Hieran cradled two mugs of dala as he negotiated a path through the stall-strewn alleys that twisted around the northeastern edge of the gardens. He passed through the gates, nodding at the two guards who stood, impassively staring out at the nest of streets. He walked quickly in spite of himself, knowing that Tehh liked his dala scalding, and hating himself for caring.

The gardens consisted almost entirely of the stunted vegetation of the north laid out precisely, with narrow, stone-covered lanes bisecting it at various intervals. He headed for the center of the gardens, where there was a sun house under the shade of a northern pine. A few guards idled along the approaching pathways, looking him over as he passed by. He wanted to stop and tell them that he was not some mere attendant sent to fetch dala by men of rank, that he was of rank himself. Tehh always had him doing menial duties that he could have had any servant perform.

Gver Keleprai and the Lastl Adept were sitting across from each other on benches in the shaded middle of the sun house, deep in discussion. Without interrupting, Hieran handed one mug over to Tehh, who did not even glance his way. The other mug was his and he stood behind Tehh, blowing on it to cool it before taking a tentative sip. Keleprai gestured for Hieran to sit, which he did, though not without a glance at Tehh.

"It is a peculiar fascination he has with these creatures, Most Gracious," Tehh was saying. "I can't say why exactly."

Hieran sipped at the dala again, and decided that his first

impression had indeed been correct and that it was wretched. He shook his head, wondering how he had not thought to taste it first before carting it back here. Tehh he saw was sipping greedily at his mug, oblivious to the dreck within. That, he knew, would not stop him from commenting on it later, Gods curse the man.

"He fears they will get the engines," Keleprai said.

"He does."

"And you do not?"

There was an edge to the Gver's voice, and Hieran nearly flinched, though he had not so much as glanced at him since gesturing for him to sit, which was just as well. It was hard to look at a man, knowing your intransigence might cost him his life. Though who was to say, he told himself. Who was to say.

"I suspect, Most Gracious, they and others will get them regardless of what we do," Tehh said with a smile. That had been his argument before the Council of Adepts in the spring, if Hieran remembered correctly.

It had been Tehh, of course, who had insisted that they meet here. He was a student of flora and always came to these gardens when he was in the capital to see what new samples had been brought south. He had declared that this was likely his only opportunity on this trip to make a visit, and, at his age, who knew when, or if, he might return to Craitol again.

Keleprai was looking away from both of them, pulling at the edges of his beard, as though he were considering what to say next. It was strange, Hieran thought, for whatever his faults, of which there were many, the Gver never lacked for words.

"He means to have us go to war. He is bringing it before the Council."

"I thought as much, Most Illustrious," Tehh said. "He will be hard pressed to win that boy the support he needs."

"Perhaps."

"The Apysel—"

"The Apysel will not stand in his way," Keleprai said.

"The tides are shifting, then."

"More than you know," Keleprai said. "More than you know."

Tehh considered this a moment. "And you will of course be supporting your Qraul in this, Most Gracious."

There was something about the way he said it that made Hieran look at him. Keleprai, he saw, had heard it too. He paused again, considering his words.

"I have agreed to what the High Adept has asked of me. I have not promised anything at the Council."

"And the Council will decide?"

"Yes."

Hieran felt the blood rush from his head. The world around them seemed to him to go still, pausing in this moment before continuing on its mad rush.

"The engines are an evil, no doubt, Most Illustrious, a blasphemy against all that the Council and the proper use of alkemya represent. But evil exists, it breeds, no doubt as fast as the Shadow Men themselves and, if we are to be rushing off to do battle against evil wherever it happens to find root, we would never rest."

Keleprai exhaled at Tehh's words. He still would not look at either of them. At last he stood and nodded at Tehh. "Thank you. I will take what you have said under advisement."

They watched him go and then Tehh turned to Hieran. "Come," he said. "There is a new thorn bush here, I am told. The northerners chew the leaves to cure stomach problems. I want a clipping of it. No doubt we will all have need of it in the days to come."

# 26

If he had been forced to put coin to the matter, Donier would have put them all on Kigarle being the Veil's man. Not only had he made it clear that Donier's inclusion in the Gver's retinue was his doing, the man had done nothing but act strangely in his presence, forever finding reason to talk with veiled meaning about his purpose here. The other night, when Kigarle had found him alone on the balcony, he had as much as told him something was going to happen to the Gver at the Council and that it would be Donier who would receive the blame.

The thought left him sick with worry, a wound he could not stanch. Wine did not work for him as it did for so many men, leaving him morose and filled with foreboding even on the best of days. There were other concoctions, of course, mythres among them, but he found no pleasure in them, just oblivion. A means to an end, he supposed, but what he truly needed was distraction. Something to cast his mind from the whirlwind of its thoughts and help to ease him into sleep.

He found it in a dancer, an enchanting girl who had attended at the celebration held for Byuvir a Kylep's arrival. Kigarle had arranged for her to see to Keleprai's needs when the Gver had found himself too much in his cups early in the evening. After his strange encounter with Kigarle that evening, Donier had run into the girl leaving the Gver's chambers as he returned to his rooms. Their eyes had linked but for a moment, the girl giving him a passing smile, and Donier had felt himself overcome with desire.

He had bowed to her and said, "Is the banquet already done?"

"It is. His Graciousness has gone to sleep."

"I would have thought a woman like you could keep him supping all night long."

The girl smiled and shook her head. "He spent so much time in his cups that his broth went cold, I am afraid, leaving me without any marrow to chew on."

Donier had offered to rectify that problem, and the dancer, laughing, had agreed. Her name was Ulrien, and a more delightful spirit Donier could not imagine. He had fallen asleep without issue following their bouts together. He had arranged to see her the following night before she left in the morning and fell upon her with an eagerness he had not felt in years when she arrived at his quarters late that evening. Something about her enchanted him deeply, whether it was her easy smile, the flash of her eyes, or the lightness of her movement, he could not say. There was something of Liene in her looks, though he knew that did not bear thinking about.

When they were through with their coupling for the moment, sharing a cup of wine, neither of them willing to sleep just yet, she began to ask him about the Gver and the Council.

"They say they mean to go to war in the desert against the Shadows, he and the High Adept."

"Where did you hear that?" he asked, studying her face carefully.

"One of the other girls heard it. Do you think it's true?"

Donier shrugged and took a sip of wine before passing the cup to her. "It's madness if it is."

"Why?" she said, her hand straying beneath the sheets to find his manhood.

"It is hopeless to fight them in the desert. They have no cities, there is nothing to attack. No land to hold. They would just strike at us as we went and melt away before we could do anything."

"But surely there must be something to be done about them? It must be so terrifying to live in the east, always under threat to them."

Donier sighed as her fingers began to work upon him. "There is nothing to be done. The Shadows are as the seasons and one cannot do battle with nature. We must find a way to live with it, storms and all."

She nodded and kissed his neck and ear. "Perhaps the High Adept can."

"No doubt he believes so," Donier said, one his hands straying to her breasts. "Why do you ask these questions?"

"These are great happenings," she said with a smile. "Is it wrong to be curious?"

"With great happenings come grave dangers, and with curiosity comes suspicion."

"You fear the days to come? You think that conjurer and your Gver will lead us all astray?" Between her words she kissed him, starting at his neck and going down his chest.

"I fear that you are a conjurer," he said, "and you have ensnared me."

She laughed and climbed astride him. "Let us see what spell we can weave together."

The mountains still loomed in the distance behind as Donier made his way along the valley floor. It seemed he was farther along than he had been at any point in his previous visions, though the valley's end was nowhere in sight. He felt like he had been walking for hours, his feet aching from blisters and his throat raw from thirst. At no point did he consider stopping, though; his footsteps were not wavering and there was nothing in sight that would shield him from the unrelenting sun.

It may have only been a trick of the light as it descended to the valley, fooling his mind into seeing something that wasn't there, but it appeared as though there was a border, hazy and not quite visible, somewhere between him and the upper reaches of the heavens where the sun made its perch. He had the odd sensation that this valley was an underworld and that the true realm lay somewhere above. That was his destination then and it could only be reached by escaping this place, wherever it was, though that would be an arduous task, for there was still no end to the horizon. A tolote, its orange-gray coat hidden amongst the scrub and earth, burst from the undergrowth to cross his path, startling him as it did. He froze and watched it go by, disappearing again into the foliage only to reappear again at various junctures as it made its way along a trail unseen by him. He gazed after it, following its loping form before starting on his way again. The creature did not turn at his movement, unusual for something so attuned to the desert, and it gave him pause. It had not even noticed him when it had crossed right before him, near enough that he might have gotten a sword on it had he had his wits about him, which was, he thought, of all of this, the strangest thing of all.

# 27

Osiphan grimaced when he saw Nyzren and her brother Bessirj clinging to his nurse's skirts, awaiting him at the entrance to their remembrance garden. He kissed his daughter in welcome and touched his son's head before leading them within. Nyzren walked beside him, which caused him to glance at her.

"What of your mother?" he whispered to her. "She refused to come?"

Nyzrella shook her head. "She is not well, father. I have assumed her duties."

Osiphan looked at her gravely and nodded, reaching out to squeeze her shoulder. "I am sorry that my mistakes have burdened you as well."

"Don't worry about me, father," she said. "Mother prepared me well for this day."

As they came near the mausoleum entrance they paused, the wet nurse stepping aside to leave the protesting Bessirj with his sister and father. Nyzren tried to comfort and quiet him. The last days would have been difficult for him, for he was still too young to begin to comprehend what was happening. There had been a brother and a sister between them, but both had died before Bessirj had been born in one of the years the plague had swept through the city. She rarely saw him, for he spent most of his days in the men's quarters of the house, under the supervision of her father's people, and he seemed not to recognize her, such was his distress.

Normally the gardens would have been filled with Ad Reteln

come to pay service to their ancestors. She wondered what they were all saying now. There would be outrage in nearly all quarters that Osiphan had ruined the family name over a failed attempt to overthrow the Ad Eselte. Would they forgive this desecration of their honor? Some would, she thought, but others would be like her mother and find forgiveness too much a burden when they were unable to meet friends' eyes on the street.

When the wet nurse had succeeded in quieting Bessirj, they entered the mausoleum, one after the other, taking a wreath of fyer from Tequihan, who stood solemn at the entrance. The circular building had but one room, a vast space with a domed roof, the center of which was open to the elements. There were four doors, one at each of the cardinal directions, including the entrance they had come through. The other three led to the tombs below. She had no idea how many tombs there were or how far below they went. Only the most trusted servants were sent into the depths to set the Reteln in their final resting place after they had lain under view for the six days and nights tradition required. The room was empty but for a simple stone icon that lay within the circle of light at the center of the room. It was an ancient thing, supposedly a likeness of the first of the Reteln, though the features had long since been smoothed away by the constant touch of fingers over the centuries.

Osiphan led them in the invocation, a standard one employed by Ceinobytes of most sects. Then they each approached the icon and placed their wreath at its feet and stroked its face. After they had shared a moment of contemplation with their ancestors, Osiphan led them all in a final invocation and they were done. It was a shorter ceremony than usual, for with only the three of them they could not perform most of the usual rites. They could only hope, as her father had said, for Hissell's forgiveness and strength.

Tequihan had set out food and wine alongside two chairs for Osiphan and Nyzren, but they barely had time to bid goodbye to Bessirj and his nurse when one of the guards arrived, bowing to both of them. Osiphan stepped aside to speak with him, and when they were done they both went away back toward the house, neither of them giving Nyzrella so much as a glance. She watched them, wondering if she should wait for her father, if he would be back soon. She glanced over at Tequihan, who shook his head.

"Do you know, Most Beautiful Husem," he said, with a

violence in his voice that she had never heard before, "that the Guard insisted on searching the mausoleum when they first came? They said we might have built tunnels to escape through there. To think that your father would disgrace his ancestors so."

Ibrazol id Ezern rose as Osiphan was ushered into the room by the guard, who saluted the Vazeir before leaving. He gestured for Osiphan to sit, which the other did, a bitter smile flashing across his lips. Ibrazol nodded, offering no formal greeting, and turned to a nearby cabinet, where one of the Reteln servants had opened a bottle of wine and left some cups. He poured out a measure in each, giving one to Osiphan, and then sat across from him.

He considered his words. "I am here out of courtesy and respect for both yourself and the Ad Reteln, whose ancestors are deserving of all the glory that has been bestowed upon them."

He paused, giving space for Osiphan to speak. He did not, and his face betrayed no emotion, though Ibrazol could feel the tension constricting his body from where he sat.

"His Most Gracious Majesty the Ad Eselte, Holder of the Realm, has pronounced on your fate. For conspiring against the Empire and his Most Immortal Majesty, you are to be banished from Darrhyn. You will spend the rest of your days in exile on your paradise in Celes."

Osiphan had gone still, his one hand clenched on the arm of his chair. "And my family, what of them?"

"They are banished as well, though, as you know, by law your wife may petition the Ad Eselte to be delivered from the bonds of marriage. If he so grants, her dowry will be returned to her. Your children are banished until they come of age, at which point they may petition the Ad Eselte as well."

"The Guard," Osiphan began to say, and then stopped. "Will we be allowed visitors?"

"They will need the permission of the Ad Eselte, but of course."

Osiphan shook his head. "And the estate?"

"The Ad Eselte has agreed to let Ephrail id Reteln determine who will inherit the estate and the family titles." Ibrazol watched him absorb this. He would know that his brother would have already come to an agreement with the Ad Eselte on how the lands would be divided. The air seemed to have gone from the room.

Osiphan licked his lips and met Ibrazol's eyes, and for a moment it seemed he would say something further. Instead he leaned back in his chair, defeated.

Ibrazol finished his wine, tossing it back in a swift motion, and stood again. "I believe that is all, Husem. The Corenedor will let you know how long you have to prepare your household."

He left without saying another word. Osiphan continued to stare into the space where he had been sitting, his wine untouched in his hand.

## 28

Gver Byuvir a Kylep and Wissier a Yseltz were discussing, in solemn tones, the Midday's rather sad display on the field, of which they had an excellent vantage point to observe from Qraul's spectator box in the pantheon. Keleprai tried to keep up with their conversation, a rather pained grin on his face. He wasn't sure whether it was the frenzy of the crowd, which on their side of the stadium was mostly for the Morning, as was the Qraul himself; the match, which he always found interminable; the fact that again he had been unable to sleep but for a few scant hours; or some combination thereof that was making the afternoon's proceedings sheer agony. Mixed with the three cups of wine he had already consumed and it was a noxious elixir.

The night before had been the worst, he decided. The days since their meeting with Attulliel had been frantic with further talks and ceremony as the other Gvers arrived. With the arrival of Hythel of Tson, all but Pervelte a Pysel had arrived. He was walking a delicate line at all times, trying to get a sense of the resolve of the others without revealing his own doubts about the High Adept's machinations. He needed to be certain of their intentions. If Pervelte smelled out his misgivings, the blood in the water at the Council would be his.

The smiling insincerity, the contrived joviality, and the manufactured concern all wore him down. Everyone acting falsely, he no less than anyone else, not a moment out of place. He had stumbled to his quarters late last night, tired beyond belief, wanting nothing more than to close his eyes and not think about what was happening and what was to be done. Least of all the path the High Adept had set them upon. But instead he lay awake, filled with a restlessness he could not place. There was no emotion, no thoughts he could not shake free from his mind, just a roving spirit that emerged from somewhere within.

Someone was speaking to him, he realized, the fog of his thoughts lifting. Wissier, the cousin of the young Gver of Yseltz.

"Are you a fan of the matches, Nes Keleprai?" he asked again, smiling awkwardly.

Byuvir, knowing him much better, laughed.

"No," Keleprai said at last, clearing his throat as he spoke. It felt like he had left his mind behind in his thoughts, his mouth flapping, useless without its motor. "I find it all baffling, to be quite honest," he added a moment later into the silence. "How anyone can grow so attached to these factions?"

"Like anything else, you are born into it," Byuvir replied. "The Akylep have been supporters of the Midday for a very long time. Much to my chagrin."

"It has been a poor these last few years," Wissier said. "Still, don't abandon us. It did not go well with us when we did."

Although Keleprai could not have been less interested, he asked what the youth was referring to.

Wissier happily responded, "Oh, this was well before my time. And yours as well."

Byuvir laughed again. "Yes, do add that. No one here was so much as a sparkle in Melinon's eye. But he will know who you are speaking of. Mad Tsivum."

Keleprai rolled his eyes in recognition. Everyone knew who Tsivum was, even if he had been dead coming on seventy-five years.

"Well, as you'll know then, Tsivum had certain theories—"

"Very certain," Byuvir interjected.

"—on many things, one of which was that no dance should have more left steps than right. And he became convinced that a particular dancer who performed one evening at court was doing just this and so he insisted that the Chair of Midday give her to his keeping, so that he might teach her a lesson for her heresy. One can only imagine what that lesson would have been."

"Something involving ardeh testicles, no doubt," Keleprai said, much to Byuvir's amusement.

"The Chair, who must have been possessed himself, actually refused Tsivum. Of course, Tsivum just had him gutted in the city square and the girl put to death and then turned his support to the Morning because it was his favourite time of day. Not six months later, he was overthrown."

He did not need to add that it was ten years before an Ayseltez would set foot again in the city, and only then with the Qraul's army behind him.

The Midday pointed just then, and both Byuvir and Wissier exploded with cheers and clapped each other on the back. Keleprai, spying an opportunity, excused himself and stepped out of the spectator box. The viewing area of the box opened into a long gallery, at the back of which food had been set out and where attendants waited to provide wine. There were a couple of side rooms that opened off the main one, and Keleprai stepped out into one of these. It led to another where the pots were, and he stepped within, handing his cup to an attendant. He fumbled a bit with his robes, which only made him more cognizant of the fact that he had taken more than his share of wine already.

Having relieved himself and retrieved his cup, he returned to the gallery. It was empty of everyone but the attendants and three dancers who were performing on a small riser near the middle of the room. Only the girl with the lute was playing, the two others taking the opportunity presented by the lack of an audience to rest and take some wine and food for themselves. He should, he thought, return to the spectator box to watch the spectacle and engage with everyone gathered there. It was important that he do so, leading into the Council in two days time, with everyone, the Gvers, their advisors, and other nobles of rank from the court, here, and Cepedutherupt absent.

He always was at such occasions, leaving the task to Keleprai or the Qraul's Master of Offices to manage. It always annoyed Keleprai, and this time he voiced his frustration to the High Adept as they had gathered after the ceremony marking the arrival of the Gver of Tson to the Council. It had been an unremarkable occasion, but the one that would follow the next day would not be. Pervelte a Pysel would arrive then. No one could say what he would do, or how the other Gvers would react. The hours that would follow would see them on the dagger's edge.

"I would only prejudice them anyway. Most of them have it in their head that I'm some fearsome creature," Cepedutherupt said to Keleprai with a dismissive wave. It was his general excuse in such matters, though it was empty reasoning. Keleprai was just as feared and despised by that mob.

He had not pressed the High Adept on the matter, knowing it to be futile. Laterala had been present as well, and he had not wanted the Qraul to see Cepedutherupt defying him. It was important that he think of Keleprai as the equal of the High Adept, whatever the truth might be. The boy failed to notice the tension between the two, though, being consumed with the Gver of Pysel and what he might do. Word of the Desu House's betrayal would have reached him by now.

"If he kills any of ours. If anyone so much as dies under suspicious circumstances, I will have him in chains for defying the Qraul's law," Laterala declared to them, his voice trembling with emotion. Keleprai noticed that his one hand was shaking as well, though he tried to hide it as his side.

"He will do nothing of the sort," Cepedutherupt replied in a matter-of-fact tone. "Not while he is at court, at your invite."

Keleprai nodded in agreement, and that seemed to satisfy the Qraul. When the boy left to see to the afternoon's arrangements, Keleprai seized the opportunity to discuss something that had been consuming his thoughts since he had met Tehh in the gardens.

"What do you think of Adept Tehh?" Cepedutherupt looked at him and Keleprai added, "I believe he may have been involved in the attack this summer."

"And what makes you think that?"

"Well, for one, his investigation turned up nothing."

"The fact that the investigation led nowhere is not evidence of guilt on the Adept's part," Cepedutherupt said. "It shows that those who organized it were very good at what they were doing. I would suggest that the investigation did point in the direction of the guilty parties. The Currlene and the Apysel, perhaps with the help of Niriese's nephew, perhaps not. And the target was surely you. That is the most simple and logical explanation."

"But he knew you would be there. And he knows the passages."

"I think that, in light of these events, it would wise for both of us to reconsider just what of ours is secret after all."

Keleprai began to respond, but Cepedutherupt raised his hand.

"He is a difficult man. He always has been. And he might betray us, that is certainly possible. But he would not betray himself doing so. He would never be associated with anyone who used the engines. Of that I am certain."

They left it there, though Keleprai could not stop thinking of what the High Adept had said: *It would be wise for both of us to reconsider just what of ours is secret after all.* Just what did that mean, he wondered? Did he suspect Keleprai of acting against him? He would put nothing past Cepedutherupt.

The assassination attempt and the failure of the investigation to turn up concrete answers bothered him. The High Adept was probably correct and it had been some manner of Apysel plot, perhaps with Niriese's family involved. He certainly could not trust her, with all that had gone between them. But there were just too many things that seemed not to fit with that theory, the use of the alkemycal engine and the strange northern musician foremost among them. The man had revealed nothing to the Chief Magister, and Keleprai had ordered his execution before leaving for Craitol.

If felt as though everything had managed to work itself beyond his grasp: the assassination and its surrounding conspiracy, the musician, his wife, and now this bizarre march to war with the High Adept. Perhaps the control he thought was his, the power to make the realms respond to his whims, was only an illusion. A young man's illusions, those, that the ceremonies and processions that placed him at the center of all being were reality when they were as much desire and hope. Now, his middle years upon him, Keleprai could not afford to indulge in such foolishness. *These days,* he thought, with no little sense of doom encompassing him, *might be my final ones before the Gods call me and all that I have wrought is left to dust.*

He suddenly realized he had been standing alone in the gallery for some time, lost in his thoughts, and that the dancers were now staring at him, while the attendants were studiously avoiding looking at him at all. He decided he was too tired for the match both on the field and in the box and, motioning for some more wine, he went to talk to the dancers.

He smiled at the girl with the lute. "I have a request, if I may."

She smiled in return and nodded. He asked for a ballad about the war, one of his favorites—a reworking of an older song from an earlier war about a common soldier who had saved a Qraul, sacrificing himself in the process. The story was neither here nor there, which was always the case. There were songs written about his exploits in the battles that had no more than a glancing touch of reality. These always seemed ridiculous to him. This song he enjoyed, though, because it pretended no relation to what had happened and the melody was light.

The girl finished the song and started another, a tavern song, one he had heard in the last year or so, though minstrels would only perform it for the public and not at court. It lacked the sophistication necessary to be played before nobles of rank, mostly because the content of the lyrics was not suitable for the ears of respectable ladies, consisting as it was of the romantic entanglements of a one-legged woman and a three-legged man. Without even thinking about it, Keleprai began to sing along and was soon joined by one of the dancers in a passable harmony. The last dancer rose to her feet and began to dance what Keleprai could only assume was her interpretation of the song's story. He laughed as they came to the verse about the two-headed man and his various escapades, which she demonstrated with aplomb.

When they had sung it home, ending in a fit of laughter, he asked her how many left steps there had been in that dance.

She laughed. "Not enough, I think, Most Gracious. Do you know that we have a dance that we call the Left Step?"

He shook his head. "You are from Yseltez?"

"I was born there, yes. My mother moved us to Craitol when I was still young. She was a dancer with the Morning too, and she taught me it."

"In honor of Nes Tsivum."

"Yes, Most Gracious" she said with a laugh. She demonstrated it for them. The other dancer quickly picked it up, and the girl with the lute provided a tune for them. Keleprai watched them, trying to follow the steps. The Yseltezi pulled him up, resisting, onto the riser and, laughing, guided him through a round. Eventually she left him to it and stepped back to admire her handiwork. They were all laughing, until finally Keleprai pulled her back into the dance. She danced across from him, her fluid movements the mirror opposite to his. She smiled all the while and his eyes never left hers.

# 29

Nyzrella had decided that she would not be kept indoors by the Imperial Guard; she would spend her afternoons in the gardens, as she always had in the days before their house arrest had begun. Those places had always been her sanctuary, and she needed them more than ever now, for the days offered no relief. Ghat and some of her mother's ladies continued to defy her, allowing him in to see her in spite of Tequihan's best efforts to keep the eunuch away. She could have them all punished, and perhaps she would still, but for the moment it seemed wiser to minimize disruption in all their lives and worry more about cultivating those allies that she would need to see them through the harder days that lay ahead.

The word of their impending exile to Celes had spread through the ranks like wildfire. Its impact would be felt everywhere, in ways that Nyzren would never have contemplated before, but would have to now. There was no need to bring all the servants and eunuchs with them to the paradise, given that it was a smaller estate and had its own retinue of servants who saw to its needs throughout the year. Some slaves would be sold to other houses and some servants would be let go to find their own way in Darrhyn. There would be those who would fear being sent from their service and those who would welcome it.

Nyzren could feel everyone's anxiety when she passed through the halls of the women's quarters and hear the muffled whispers that followed in her wake, for they all knew who ruled the household now. She had set Tequihan and Quesin with the task of providing a list of those servants whom she could trust, those whom she needed regardless, and those who could be safely left when they went into exile. Among that last group she was certain would lie Ghat and those of her mother's ladies who persisted in defying her. She had also told Tequihan to determine how it was Ghat continued to have access to whatever concoction it was he provided Usyre, for she remained insensible and in a state of oblivion to which Nyzren could not reach.

It was Bausch, the kitchen boy Kenul sent out each day to procure their sustenance, who was to blame, Nyzren was certain, for no one else was allowed to leave the Ad Reteln grounds. The only other possibility was that Ghat had somehow bought the favor of one of the Guard, but what did he have to offer?

It was concerns such as these that kept her own fears at the impending exile at bay. She had spent little time dwelling on what it would mean for her, beyond the fact that she would most certainly be commanding the women's quarters in Celes, at least until Usyre had recovered her senses, if she ever did. That thought filled her with such rage that Nyzren found herself pacing about the gardens instead of sitting in contemplation of the wisdom of Sage Nuerrallah as she had intended. She could not decide what it was about Ghat that infuriated her most: his general insolence, his defiance of her commands, or the insufferable arrogance of his expression when he was in her presence. Let him think that he had achieved some victory over her for the moment, she thought, and he would find out how just how hollow that victory was.

As she was walking, lost in thought and without direction, one of the Guard appeared on the path ahead of her. He had waited, she noted, until she was in the midst of the grove of citrus trees on the eastern edge of the grounds, near the mausoleum, where any encounter would be obscured from prying eyes. She felt her heart lurch in her chest and cursed herself for sending Quesin back to the house. While she wondered if she should cry out or turn and run, the man glanced about, to assure himself they were alone, and approached her, raising his hands as though to submit to her. It was enough to keep her where she stood, though it did little to calm her.

"Do not run, Husem" the guard whispered as he came close. "We must have words."

Nyzren did not bother to tell him that she could not have fled even if she wanted to; her legs were trembling so badly that she feared she would fall if she attempted to. "Speak," she said, in what she hoped was a commanding voice.

The guard nodded and said, "Tell your father to come here tomorrow at this time. I will be waiting for him."

"Why should he wish to share words with one who so falsely imprisons him?" she found herself saying. Where, she wondered, had all this spirit come from in these last days?

The guard had already started past her, heading back to the wall. "He will want to hear what I have to say," he said as he went. Nyzren watched him go, staying where she was until her legs ceased there shaking and the breath returned to her lungs and she was able to go on her way.

The guard was waiting for him at the appointed hour, just as Nyzrella had said he would be, loitering uneasily in amidst the citrus trees heavy with fruit. Osiphan caught sight of him a moment before the man realized he was there and stood watching as the guard fidgeted and glanced behind him, his nerves worn plain upon his face. Seeing that set him at ease, and he continued on, his movement at last drawing the guard's attention. Osiphan noted with approval that all trace of anxiety vanished from the man's expression as soon as he caught sight of the Nohritai, and by the time they came face to face, the guard projected only the calm reserve that always seemed to mark their kind.

"Thank you for seeing me, Husem," the guard said by way of greeting. Osiphan did not reply, waiting for the man to say his piece. "I bring word from our shared stout acquaintance."

"And what does he say?"

The guard glanced about him again, as though still not trusting that they were alone. Osiphan did not take his eyes from the man's face. "There is little to tell and little to be done. Our imperial brother remains untouched. Our Sage is still pure of belief. Those are the cards to be played."

Osiphan nodded and turned away from the guard, staring back toward the mausoleum, asking his ancestors for guidance. The boy Masiph could be of use. Revealing his involvement to Ibrazol would offer some satisfaction if nothing else, but Osiphan was reluctant to do that. Now was not the time to waste on petty vengeance and, if by some miracle the boy rose in rank in the coming years, he would be of much more utility.

"Did he say anything of the emissary?" Osiphan said to the guard, who shook his head. What, he wondered, could the Craitolians want? Why send an emissary in secret if they did not have some scheme or alliance in mind? He desperately wanted to know whether this was a singular event. Had there been others? Would more follow? The Ad Eselte and the Vazeir were consumed solely by their own power, they would welcome the alkemya mongers with open arms if they stood to benefit, no matter the corruption to the Empire. His best course of action, then, was to thwart them in this, since he could not hope to shake them free from their perches.

He turned to the guard. "Tell our mutual friend that our Sage should find opportunity to bless the emissary."

The guard bowed and turned on heel, going quickly from the grove. Osiphan lingered for a time after the sound of the man's footsteps had disappeared, drawing in breaths heavy with scent of citrus. There would not be many days left when he might take such pleasures in the place that had been his home for all his days, and he intended to seize what he could.

# 30

The carriers picked their way carefully through the darkness, the heavens obscured by clouds and first light still hours away. There was the smell of rain on the air, a hint of what might await them when day arrived. One of the guards—there were three with the palanquin—stumbled and cursed softly. The road they were on was obscure and poorly kept, making it a struggle for everyone to maintain their footing.

They had left the walls of Craitol nearly two hours before, slipping out one of the minor gates where prostitutes, thieves, and others of less-than-sterling reputation would pay off the guard to pass in or out of the city. A palanquin guarded by three hired swords might seem to be something a little out of the ordinary, given the usual comings and goings at the gate, but, in fact, it was not all that rare that the wealthy or powerful were forced them to leave Craitol under less than ideal circumstances. Those on duty at the gate knew only too well that it was best for their continued well-being if they did not pay much mind to who was passing by.

After passing through the gate, the palanquin followed a winding path through the slums outside the wall onto a series of old roads and pathways that led south of the city. The carriers did not know who their passenger was. They were slaves, bought in the market the morning before by a man dressed in the robes of some Sentuerist sect and brought to a cloister. They had been fed and allowed to sleep through the day, and were woken only once the sun had gone from the sky. The palanquin sat in the courtyard of the cloister, brought while the carriers had slept, and by the time they came to hoist it to their shoulders, their passenger was already within. The three swords had been there as well, the man who had purchased the slaves nowhere to be seen, and with a minimum of discussion they set out.

Alieren was almost ecstatically pleased at how well it had gone. Of course, they still had to return, and that might prove more difficult. And there was the meeting that still lay ahead, which would prove the most troublesome of all. For the moment she reveled in all the planning come to fruition, to escape not just the palace, but the city as well, without anyone being the wiser. She was so excited that she managed to mostly ignore the cold, though her fingers were beginning to grow a bit numb. It was a very autumnal morning, foreshadowing the seasons' change that lay a little more than a month away.

There was sharp jolt and the palanquin lurching off kilter, spilling Alieren from the bench and very nearly from the carriage itself. One of the carriers grunted and swore in pain and was silenced by Het with a harsh word and a blow. She got herself into her seat again, the palanquin having only momentarily halted in its progress, and thought that it would just be her luck to injure herself her first time out of the capital since her arrival.

She was just beginning to grow nervous that Het had somehow missed the meeting place when he called for a halt. He whistled the call of a fedaz sucker twice and waited for a response. None was forthcoming, so they waited, worry and fear churning through her as she thought of all the various reasons that might explain why the man she was to rendezvous with was not already here. None was satisfying in the least. Ten minutes passed and then another ten. The men outside the carriage started to get restless, shifting about. She began to think how cruel fate was that she should get this far only to be stymied by the one thing she had assumed was assured.

At last two whistles came from somewhere behind them. Het waited a moment, in which Alieren nearly yelled at him before replying in kind. One of the guards led the carriers away from the palanquin so that they would not see who was approaching. She waited, overwhelmed by equal parts anticipation and trepidation. Footsteps approached the palanquin and Het spoke in a low voice, something she couldn't make out. There was a reply and the curtain to the carriage was pulled back and Gver Pervelte a Pysel stepped inside and sat across from her.

"My apologies for my tardiness, Most Gracious," he said. "I wanted to make certain you hadn't been followed."

"And were we, Nes Pervelte?" she asked, with more of an edge to her voice than she had intended.

She thought she saw the outlines of a smile on his face. "No, Most Gracious. No indeed."

He had left the curtain open in the middle, which dispelled a bit of the gloom that she had journeyed in, though it was hardly lighter outside. Their respective guards had taken up positions around the palanquin outside of the range of their voices. She turned back to the Gver, striving to get a sense of what he was thinking, but it was impossible, his face drowned in the depths of the night. He was stretched out easily on the bench, leaning as far back from her as he could, so that all she could really discern were the outlines of his form, including the absence where his left arm should have been.

"I am sorry to see the distant rumors we hear in Pysel confirmed here."

"And what would those be?" she said, dispensing with formality as he had.

"Well, your presence here must mean that our illustrious Qraul does not occupy your keep. Perhaps you are a salamander and have your jewels well armored. Still, I'm surprised the High Adept is not standing sentinel to ensure you are well seeded."

"The gossip of the Realm is hardly what I wanted to discuss with you."

He appeared not to have heard her. "Perhaps your husband needs more study on the matter. He is young and unlearned, after all. He would do well to pass some time in your city's fine academies."

She bit off a retort, knowing he was goading her with his coarseness.

"My apologies, Most Glorious," Pervelte said. "I had no intention to harm. If the wound is deep, I have the balm for it. I could inoculate you here and satisfy not only your appetite, but the High Adept's as well."

"You have no lust for my spoils," she said. "You just want to see the High Adept's face when you tell him that your spawn is in line for the throne."

He laughed. "That is true."

"But I did not risk all this for a mere ramble."

He was silent a moment. "I am impressed. Most impressed."

Alieren decided their wit was leading nowhere, and it was not as though they had the luxury of time. After all, he was to be presenting himself to court later that day and she would have to be there to receive him.

"We both know that tomorrow the High Adept will propose a war against the Shadow Men when you sit in Council. I think we can agree that right thinking people of this Realm must do whatever we can to stop such a rash act."

"I might agree with you, but as I'm sure you're aware, I am not at present in a position to oppose whatever the High Adept might propose. Nor are you, if it comes to that."

"On that you are not correct," she said, hoping she sounded more confident than she felt. "My husband can be made to see reason on this. Provided the word comes from someone he trusts."

"You are his counsel-keeper, are you? The word one hears is that his mother has ensnared him in her quagmire, not you."

"Many do say that. The High Adept believes it. But I have his ear and I know otherwise."

"He is your drudge, is he? Sweet on your delight."

Alieren decided that a response to that was beneath the dignity of her office. He was nothing like she had been led to expect from the stories that were told in court. Those portrayed the Gver of Pysel as a depraved menace, a man who had fed on his resentment and grievance until there was only a stub of rage left to his soul. They said he had never been the same after returning without an arm from a war he had neither supported nor believed in, and had in fact counseled Lestulatera against.

He had been at court twice in her five years there, once for her wedding and two years later for the Council of All Gvers. Neither of those times had he said anything to her beyond the formalities required of him. But that stood to reason: her marriage had been for him the final straw, the last betrayal of the High Adept and the Alastl. From that moment he had cast himself totally against the Qraul, working not to gain influence in his court but to overthrow him. The last five years had in effect seen the Realm suffused in a subterranean conflict that at all times threatened to burst into the light of day.

It was because of those continued hostilities, which she was irretrievably enmeshed in, that she could not trust that the man before her was the real Pervelte. The stories of his anger and violence might be exaggerated, but there were enough real casualties that she knew they were not outright lies. So she had to be extremely careful here and not let his insults provoke her, no matter how difficult that might be, for who knew what he might do in turn?

"I can convince him of the error in this," she started again. "There is no benefit to him in this war. There is no benefit for anyone, near as I can tell, though the High Adept must have his reasons."

"Oh, he does," the Gver said, not elaborating any further.

She decided to wait for him to speak and, when he finally did, there was a trace of amusement in his voice.

"So let us assume for the moment that you do have the ear of the Qraul. That you can whisper to him of endless delights that await him from your spinning and the tapestries you shall make. And not only that, but that you have enough influence to turn him against the wishes of the High Adept and the fool of Lastl. If you can do this, what need do you have of me?"

He was mocking her, not giving her any consideration at all. Why had he agreed to this meeting, with so much effort and risk involved for both of them?

"I can make him see the foolishness of this, but, even if I do, he will not turn from Cepedutherupt and Keleprai. Unless…unless he knows that he has the full support of the other Gvers. He will not stand alone. He cannot. But with the other Gvers, with the Apysel, behind him. What could Cepedutherupt and Keleprai do in the face of that? Defy the Qraul? Go to war against the Realm once more? Keleprai does not have the stomach for that, even if the High Adept does."

There was a long pause and a marked stillness from the man sitting across from her. For the first time since he had entered the palanquin, Alieren had the sense that he was not smiling, not humoring her. She allowed a tiny measure of hope to steal into her mind. As the silence stretched on, she glanced outside at the darkness, noticing for the first time the quiet that hung over everything, vast and impenetrable.

"So you offer nothing, then. The support of a puppet. And the rest is left to me, I suppose, to conjure the support of the Gvers from thin air.

"The Qraul is a child and he will do what he is told," Pervelte continued. "And children are used to being told what to do by their nurses. So he might very well take the word of the one he is enseamed with. He might very well. It matters little in the end."

She swallowed the emotion boiling inside her and said, "If the Gvers know that the Qraul might abandon the High Adept and Lastl…"

"And I, sworn enemy of the Qraul, am going to come to them with a tale that the Qraulla has promised me the support of the Qraul if only they will support me. What will they believe?"

"I could speak to them."

He waved his hand. "It cannot be done."

"I got you here, did I not?" she said, letting some of the heat she felt enter her voice.

"You intrigued me, no doubt. Perhaps you will do the same with the others. Perhaps. However. I will not give my support."

"Why?" she asked, her voice barely a whisper. She felt as though she had been struck.

"I will never give my support to a Lestulatyr or whatever children Melinon may grace you with. Any chance of that happening ended the day you married the boy."

"That was not his choice, nor was it mine."

"Of course. It was Cepedutherupt's. And Keleprai's. A final insult after a war against the Realm itself."

"I know this," Alieren said. "It was my people against whom the war was waged, remember. But must Laterala pay for the mistakes of others? Isn't this a chance for a righting of that wrong?"

"There is no righting it," Pervelte said, his voice heavy with an undercurrent of violence. After a moment he continued, the amusement returning to his voice. "This has nothing to do with either he or you. He is a puppet, nothing more. You may want to pull the strings, but so long as the High Adept holds the Council, you will not."

"You would do this even though it will mean the Realm will go to war."

"I want this war. The cost to me is nothing. A few men. The cost to the High Adept and Keleprai, though, if it is a failure, a disaster? They will be weakened. Even with the Desu whoresons' coin, this will cost them greatly. Nothing short of triumph will repay the expense. Even then. They are not the only ones able to make friends with the Enir.

"No, it is clear. Right now, without the Desu House, it is better for my family if this war happens. You speak of the good of the Realm, but you are confusing the good of the Realm with what is good for the Qraul. And for you. They are not the same. For long enough the cabal that stands behind Laterala, and his father before him, have driven the Realm toward ruin. There is need of a cleansing. I will not rest until I have destroyed them and there is a new rule in the land."

Alieren shivered as he said the last, for he was clearly speaking of her destruction as well. The fierce urgency with which he said those last words was both terrifying and fascinating in equal measure. Here at last, she thought, was the man. He would have his vengeance. She could not think of anything to say.

Pervelte rose to his feet and stepped out of the carriage, their discussion at an end. He turned to her. "You had better not dally any more with me or they will suspect you are in revolt. If I were you, I would consider it. If you are not with child soon enough, the High Adept will see that a more suitable venture is obtained. You are not the only coin for stamping in this Realm. I recommend a banquet with as many attendants as you can manage."

Tears stung her eyes as the emotion that she had kept contained through their conversation threatened to come to the fore, and she was glad for the darkness that he was not able to see that he had made his mark. She heard him issue an order as he left, and soon Het was at the side of the palanquin, pulling the curtains shut.

"We shall have to go quickly, Most Gracious," he said.

She did not reply, and the carriers were soon there lifting the palanquin and starting her on her homeward journey. The tension and excitement of the first half of the journey had disappeared, replaced by despair. When she returned, when she had some food and sleep, perhaps she would find her strength of will again. This battle was not done, she told herself. She would not let it end here in the ashes of Pervelte's bitterness. For now she trusted that Het would see to the details of their return, including the slaves who could not be allowed to see the light of day.

She thought of Cepedutherup and what he wanted with this desert invasion. Pervelte had known, or thought he did, but she had no idea. Any of the soldiers she had spoken with had told her the same thing: that an invasion of the desert was untenable. The Shadow Men would not stand to fight, the creatures had no cities, no fortresses to defend. They were nomads. They would simply drift away, leading their armies deeper and deeper into the desert, attacking whenever the opportunity presented itself.

The High Adept knew this. He knew as well as Pervelte the potential price to be paid. He knew that the peace and stability he had just bought at home were illusory, and that as soon as the Craitolian armies returned from the desert, assuming any did, the shadow war with the Apysel would begin anew. The only explanation, she thought, was that he does not care if Laterala remained as Qraul, or whether or not his own influence within the Realm waned. Whatever lay in the desert was more important. And Pervelte knew it too and could afford to bide his time.

In the north they spoke of a creature, a demon called an abapolly. It was a holdover from the age when Kragians had worshiped their own gods, before Craitol had conquered them entirely, and so the cureders frowned on any belief in it. But the common folk, and many nobles of rank if truth be told, continued to tell stories of it and to make offerings in their places. They were said to inhabit caves and crevices, or live inside mountains, any entrances to the earth's depths that might lead to Ulternon's Hall. The story that she was most familiar with told of a sorcerer who had been scorned by the woman he loved and who, in an attempt to impress and win her back, had called forth an abapolly, enslaving it with alkemya. The sorcerer had the demon exact vengeance upon the man who had stolen his beloved, and then used the creature's powers to gain wealth and influence beyond all imagining. It could not be controlled, of course, and in the end the sorcerer came to ruin and death, with his beloved taken by the creature back to its underworld realm.

It was just a tale and it was always foolish to see larger things in a story told to frighten her to bed as a child. But Cepedutherupt was very much an abapolly, and she felt very certain, now more than ever, that this war which Laterala so desperately wanted would lead to his ruin, and hers as well.

# FOUR:

# MADNESS IN ALL REALMS

# 31

Alieren and Laterala walked arm in arm down the long aisle that led to the Council Hall, flanked on either side by the court of Craitol and the Gvers of the Realm with all their attendants, flags and other regalia on full display. When they reached the door, the Sanader of the city blessed them both in the name of the Three and the Kedaui Guard, who always stood before the Council doors, swung them open and allowed the Qraul and Qraulla to enter the empty room. They were followed by a flourish of trumpets and two Heralds as they moved past the individual boxes the Gvers would occupy and went up the steps to sit beside each other on their thrones. One of the Heralds followed them and went to stand on the riser below, while the other sat at a table near the middle of the hall, where he would best be able to hear the speeches that would follow, preparing his scrolls to record the proceedings.

As the first Herald began to announce the Gvers, each of whom entered the Council Room and prostrated himself before the Qraul and Qraulla before occupying their box, Alieren studied her husband out of the corner of her eye. Though he affected to sit impassively, watching the proceedings, she knew him too well to be fooled by that. He had waited years for the day when he might seize the Realm and direct its energies, proving to those assembled that he was no mere boy Qraul.

Though she had no standing, no one in this room to support her, Alieren had, the night before, at last summoned the nerve and tried to put proof to her claims that she could turn her husband with her persuasion and charm. As he had every night since the Gvers had begun arriving for the Council, he came to their chambers, the necessity of getting his wife with child before he left for war pressing him.

He was in an ecstatic mood when she received him, already imagining his return to the gates of Craitol, a cheering throng to greet him. It seemed the High Adept had given him word that Gver Pervelte would not oppose them. That was not news to Alieren, but she said nothing as Laterala exulted in his triumph.

"That leaves the rest of the Council, and Cepedutherupt controls that."

"Yes he does," she said.

"So it won't be a problem. I can't believe how easy it has been, actually. I would have thought that Pervelte would stand up to us, but I guess he lost the stomach for the fight."

"Perhaps."

He raised his head to look down at her, smiling indulgently at her. "Come on. What is it? You've your own theory, I'm sure."

"Well," she said, trying to think how best to say it, "maybe he sees nothing to gain in stopping you from going ahead, and something to gain if you do."

"What could that be?"

She took his hand in both of hers and looked at him directly. "What if you lose this war?" He opened his mouth to say something to her, but she stopped him. "Or what if you win? What if you return, but the victory is not decisive? Think of it. All that coin spent and the mercenary companies will need to rebuild and recruit. The Apysel can stand aside, and when you return, whatever strength we have gained with these new alliances will be lost."

She was quiet, letting her words sink in. Laterala thought on it for a tantalizingly long time. "All you have is the High Adept's claims. Who is to say that he knows all realms?"

He shook his head. "Keleprai is in agreement as well. This is a wise course."

The Gver of Lastl was a godsforsaken fool, she wanted to say. He was as much a mouth of the High Adept as Laterala. But she did not have it in her to be ruthless with him, as she would have needed to in order to turn him from this path. Laterala was far too innocent, too ignorant of the harder realities of the Realm, and he had yet to be bloodied by any of life's disappointments. Those days would come—perhaps soon, she knew—but she did not give voice to those worries either as he began to kiss her breasts, his desire pressing him on again.

The High Adept had that in him, of that she had no doubt. He had proven this so countless times, and he would do so again this day before them all. These were her thoughts, of the bitterness of her pleasure, perhaps the last for her to come in some time, as Cepedutherupt approached and abased himself before them and then rose and turned to speak to those assembled.

As the High Adept praised the balance of this realm, and the three Gods who oversaw it and all that their creatures on this earth did, Keleprai tried to settle his mind, which was vibrating between a coursing, singing energy and the utter desolation of exhaustion. It had been a sleepless night, one racked by anguish, and he had not been alone to judge by the faces of the others gathered with him. All but the High Adept, who maintained his serene bearing as he continued with the interminable invocations that opened every Council.

Keleprai paid no mind to it, studying the other Gvers, each of them in their box with their advisors and attendants behind them. The oldest Gvers sat nearest the Qraul's throne, so Pervelte was beside him and Byuvir and Duirhe a Takyl sat immediately across. There were nine of them in all, with the northern nobles not being summoned, and each of them would have the opportunity to speak once the High Adept was finished. The Qraul did not speak, for in its earliest days, when the Gvers had first forced the Council upon the Qraul, it had served as a forum to allow the Great Families to bring their grievances where the Qraul would have to listen. As the Qraul's power in the Realm waned, it became the place where he had to come to gain the Gvers' approval for his taxes and his wars, and so it became necessary to have someone to speak of the Qraul's behalf on the business of the day. It was the High Adept who did so now, standing where he had ten years earlier, uttering the same empty words, the Gvers paying no heed to any of it.

Everyone knew, after all, what Cepedutherupt was going to say, what the Qraul was going to ask of them. What was to happen now, during the endless speechifying that would take place this day, was the outcome of the vote that would follow when all talk was through. The truth would come out after so many days of withholding and obfuscating, each Gver having nodded in this direction and that, with no words put to any oath. All but Keleprai; he alone had stood beside his Qraul, though his heart held different words.

Tehh yawned from his chair behind his right shoulder and Keleprai was suddenly aware of all the dim noises of the room, the shifting of robes and chairs, the scratch of quill on parchment. The last did not come from the Herald recording the High Adept's words alone, the Gvers had begun their scrivening. No one knew when the custom had begun—perhaps it had existed from the very beginnings of the Council—but it had long been the case that while speeches were made, the business of the Realm was settled by the Gvers and the High Adept in silence, by the passing of notes. When Lusighyral had rebuilt the Council Hall after fires had nearly consumed the entire palace, during the Hitazi Riots, he had acknowledged practice and made it custom by constructing the boxes that each Gver sat in, providing an exit into the surrounding corridors where the Gvers' emissaries could exchange notes and trade words.

The corridors would be filled with any number of courtiers and hangers-on, each Gver sending agents out to intercept their rivals or otherwise gain advantage. Laterala's Master of Offices would be there as well, along with other agents of the Qraul, to keep the peace and speak for his interests. As a result, there was something of an art to the passing of notes, especially given that it was nearly impossible to disguise which of the Gvers were exchanging words. It was not unknown for an emissary to lose a note on his way to deliver it and in some cases, where theft failed, the situation escalated to murder.

"We gather here today, for a shadow has fallen across the land. If we are honest with ourselves, it has lain across our existence for far too long. We live in fear, a fear that curdles the stomach and slouches the shoulders. We have reached that moment, that precipice, where we must strike against the Shadows while the opportunity presents itself or forever submit to them and their predations."

The day's first note, marked with the Akylep seal, arrived at that moment, Tehh's Disciple stepping forward to hand it to him. It read, in Byuvir's careless hand: *Did I not have your promise for your son's hand?*

Keleprai was careful to suppress a smirk as he read it, for he had done no such thing. There had been talks, but there were always talks among the Great Families, and very few formal agreements. What Byuvir wanted was for his acquiescence on this and his part in the war to be paid for. It was a standard tactic in these Councils, when Gvers knew their support was needed, to squeeze for every piece of coin they could manage. The expected response would be for him to apologize and ask what could be done to salve this grievance. Then they would come to terms and Byuvir would support the Qraul.

That was not what he did. Turning to his left, where there was a small writing table, Keleprai took up his quill and wrote: *In such a dire time, such small concerns as these should not distract us from the matter of the day.* He folded the note and pressed his seal upon it, passing it behind him to Hieran to be delivered. The hour is not so late, he thought. Let us see what will come.

*Let Senteur come, his hand from the heavens, casting every godsforsaken one of them aside.* Hieran passed from the corridor leading into Gver Keleprai's box, where servants idled awaiting a command from their master, and out to the maelstrom of the halls surrounding the Council chambers, his mood black. Drabs and whoresons the lot of them, he thought, as he dodged among the scurrying servants and the various hangers-on milling about, no doubt trying to discern who was passing notes among the Gvers. A waste of time, the whole thing, for Pervelte was apparently not going to stand against the proposal and Keleprai, for all his talk with Tehh, would not dare turn from the High Adept, Hieran was certain. For the rest of the Gvers, they would happily go along for whatever baubles or trinkets the Qraul offered, like any common trull.

He followed the broad corridor around to where it narrowed slightly, curving around the Qraul's throne, before expanding again as it ran along the chamber's far side. Gver Byuvir's box was the first on this side, for which he was glad. He could hand the note off and be out of the insufferable melee, where everyone was watching everyone with guarded stares, a thousand conspiracies suspected.

It was not to be. Before he even made it past the Qraul's corner, Fedyl Kugisyr emerged from the crowd and grasped him by the shoulder, pulling him aside to one of the half columns that jutted out from the walls.

"Are you enjoying your service, Hieran?" Fedyl said, smiling like poison come for dinner. They had studied at the Council together, Fedyl never showing much promise, failing the tests and being cast to the Council's outer circle. He had become an agent for Adept Weirn, one of the many faceless men in the service of the Council Adepts, practicing thaumaturgy in villages, finding promising students, or, as in the case of Fedyl, becoming a man who did those things Adepts wanted done without their having to do it.

Vile creature, Hieran thought. "Not so much as you I expect. You always favored abuse, as I recall."

"Strange that you are the one at all fours for your master, then."

"At least I don't have a taste for the marrow of the bone."

"I see your lips are as whore-rotted as your eyes."

Hieran waved a dismissive hand at him. "I have no time for you. People of consequence await me."

"Just as you had no time this summer when you were searching for your Gver's attacker blind as any piss-burnt man."

"I had little to do with that."

"Little indeed. An engine in the Gver's chamber. And who do you think put it there?"

Hieran frowned, wondering if this was just talk or if there was any meat on this bone. He was distracted for a moment by the sight of a servant, in the court's colors, watching them. Before he had a chance to wonder why, the man glanced at someone in the passing crowd and this man, also in the Qraul's colors, but a peninsular by his shade, stepped out from the mass and clamped a hand across Fedyl's mouth, pulling his head back, and said, "Wanton lips, Fedyl Kugisyr. Today the Veil is lifted."

As Fedyl struggled to free himself, the peninsular raked a dagger across his throat, so quickly that Hieran wondered whether it had even touched him. Blood began to issue from the wound in thick rivulets, and Fedyl grasped at his throat as though he might stanch it, his mouth opening and closing soundlessly, except for a slight gasping, as though his lungs could not draw any air. The man released him, dropping the dagger to the ground and disappearing into the crowd as seamlessly as he had materialized. Fedyl took a step forward and then fell, and Hieran moved involuntarily to catch him, lowering him to the ground where he struggled frantically, blood leaching from him at a frightening rate.

There were gasps from those around him, everyone suddenly noticing what had happened, the murderer already vanished. A few courtiers stood by, stupidly looking on as though unsure of what to do. While he watched Fedyl die, Hieran kept an eye on all those gathering around and, when one of the Kedaui Guard arrived, he was able to point out the servant who had given the signal, for he had stayed at the back of the crowd to see the deed through to its end.

## 32

From the corner of his eye, Keleprai could see Gver Pervelte as he sat in his box, leaning his head against his one good hand, looking as though he had all the time in the Realm. Which he did, if it came to that; he had all of existence to wait for Laterala, Cepedutherupt, and Keleprai to go and break themselves against the rocks of the desert. They walked such a fine line in all of this, even now with the Desu coin to back them. It would not take much to exhaust it, and when it was, the Gvers who now sent him notes would be sending them to Pervelte. All for the Shadows and the alkemycal engines. Madness, madness that might shake loose the center of the Realm.

The notes had piled up since he had sent that cursed Disciple to Byuvir. Duirhe was asking for Lastl to provide soldiers for five of pyrsedies, a steep price indeed, while Issilar a Yseltez and Hythel a Tson wanted only the hand of one of his nieces and favorable terms on some coin from the Suher House respectively. All easily done if it came to that, but not if he were to continue on the path he had set with his note to Byuvir. There was no turning aside now, with Byuvir's furious response no doubt moments away from arriving, and yet he still hesitated to take up the quill, to do what must be done.

"Why now, at this moment, is such action necessary, you ask," Cepedutherupt was saying. "It must be now, or our hands will be stilled by the creatures themselves. The Shadows have the engines and they have the knowledge of the things. The Council cannot allow their power to grow, cannot allow them the use of these things, which you know as well as I are against balance of the Gods. It must be now."

The stirring of the attendants behind him alerted Keleprai to Hieran's return. No note was passed forward, though, and after a moment he heard Tehh rise from his seat, retreating to the corridor to conference with his Disciple. He risked a glance back and saw the Disciple earnestly whispering something to the Adept. One of the attendants brought a note forward, written faintly in Tehh's spidery hand: *Murder at Qraul's corner. Golden Veil. More to follow?*

He felt his mouth go dry. He wrote a quick reply, but when he turned to hand it to the attendant he saw that Tehh and the Disciple had already gone.

Donier's mouth was dry and he longed for some water to quench his thirst, but he dared not leave his post at the entrance to the Gver's box. Kigarle stood across from him, both of them staring grimly out at the ever-shifting crowd of attendants and courtiers, any one of whom might be an agent of the Veil. So, in his own way, was he, Donier realized, though he did not know what part he would be asked to play. It seemed evident that it would come on this day with the distraction of the Council and so many men gathered in the corridors of the Qraul's Palace that a strange face here or there would attract no notice.

The man across from him was, he was now certain, part of the Veil conspiracy as well. Kigarle had rarely left his side during the celebration the night before in welcome of Gver Pervelte. It had been as though they were newly betrothed, Kigarle the nervous husband who did not quite trust his wife in mixed company. Everything he said seemed to hint at their dark alliance and the foul deeds that would follow from it. He had left the celebration as soon as politeness allowed and awaited Ulrien in his rooms, working his way through the better part of a bottle of wine.

Such was his growing paranoia that he briefly suspected the dancer of being an agent of the Veil, though if she was she had already wasted her opportunity to murder Gver Keleprai. Her continual questions about the machinations and shifting alliances before the Council had roused his suspicions, and no matter how many times he told himself that it was no more than youthful curiosity—the girl had never been called to attend at the palace before, after all—he could not quell his growing doubt. It did not stop him from seeing her that night or for ensuring that she would call on him after the Council was done this day. If anything, it only served to spur his already insatiable desire for her.

Donier's thoughts drifted into a reverie over last night's pleasures, his gaze casting vacantly over the passersby in the corridor. Tehh's Disciple appeared from within the crowd, thrusting himself between he and Kigarle and into the Gver's box. As the Disciple passed them, Donier thought he could see blood on his hands and robe, though he could not be entirely certain. He turned and watched the man whispering to one of the Gver's attendants, and when he turned back Kigarle was staring at him with an unreadable expression. Donier shivered and whirled to face the corridor, certain now that something was about to happen.

A moment later, the Adept and the Disciple emerged behind them and Donier could see that it was blood, without a doubt, that marked the Disciple. Adept Tehh looked from Donier to Kigarle, his eyes stern, though his lips seemed to hint at a smile.

"Let no one through but my Disciple or myself," he told them. "Any attendants bringing notes must pass them to you. Do you understand?"

Both Kigarle and Donier nodded. "Good. Be wary. The Veil has returned," Tehh said, gesturing at the blood on his Disciple, "and I fear they have only just begun."

The Adept strode off into the crowd, his Disciple in tow, disappearing after a moment. Donier watched him go before turning again to face Kigarle, who met his gaze, his expression unchanging. Neither of them spoke, both turning to face the corridor again, waiting for what would happen next.

"It must be now," Cepedutherupt said for the third or fourth time in his speech while Alieren envisaged garroting him from behind, like one of those insidious northern females who always populated southern romances, vixens who seduced and led nobles astray only to reveal, late in the play, the murder that lay in their hearts. Today that was not her role. No, today she was to be a symbol of the Realm, to sit and represent it with her husband in all its balance and glory. A silent icon, untouched by the grime of what was occurring below: the bartering of souls.

"It must be now, because we have an opportunity to rid

ourselves of twin scourges, both of which have long plagued this great Realm. Kercubegahedd's minions, those who still remain, are spreading out to all realms, and they will stop at nothing to ensure that the engines and their knowledge survive. And that includes trade with the Shadows."

The High Adept paused to let his words sink in to those assembled, which was amusing because none of the Gvers—the ones who would ultimately cast their votes, after all—would be paying him any mind. They were too busy ardeh trading and worse; no doubt the knives were out in the corridors around the Council, everyone struggling for the higher hand. A Council of Shadows in truth, consumed by them and carried out in them. Only the attendants, the Herald, and she and the Qraul, those who were bound by duty to listen, were doing so.

The talk of Kercubegahedd worried her, for the only thought that had provided any salve to her anguish about this was that at least this time the north would be spared any bloodshed. But perhaps the war in the desert was not the end in itself, but a mere prelude to another in the north. And why not? They were the death's mirror of the Shadow Men, after all; even she who had a Craitolian shade, more or less, was assumed to be tainted with that ghostly pallor.

"One of my agents has infiltrated their ranks," the High Adept continued. "He was able to send me images of the engines the Shadows have collected in one of the imperial ruins. It is a disturbing number, I can assure you, and he made clear that the creatures have more than a rudimentary understanding of how to use them. They menace our borders now without the aid of alkemya. Imagine what they could become with it."

Imagine, Alieren thought. That she could easily do. She could imagine Laterala roaming the desert for a decade under the lashing of the High Adept, parsing each grain of sand for the engines, always another to be found, everyone gone well mad by the time they returned home to find the Realm in Pervelte's hands.

# 33

In the last days, Masiph had been unable to shake the sense that he was being followed. The blissful respite he had enjoyed since the end of the conspiracy against the Ad Eselte, and his miraculous escape, vanished in an instant, to be replaced by confusion and anxiety. At no point had he seen any pursuers, though he was not fool enough to believe that meant anything. He tried to dismiss the feeling as nothing more than paranoia, the ill humor resulting from his involvement in Osiphan's plot, but it had become so pervasive that he could only conclude there was something to it. His ancestors were clearly trying to warn him of something, though what he could not say. He had, as best he could tell, escaped the conspiracy without suffering any consequences, though he supposed both Osiphan and Nazeed had cards left to play. Other than those two, he could not fathom why anyone would be following him. It certainly wouldn't be the Guard; if they suspected him of something they would simply arrest him.

Perhaps, he told himself, it was simply his guilt at the murder of the administrator manifesting itself at last. That he had felt nothing following those terrible events, had barely given the man another thought, struck him as strange given his difficulties following the raid. There had been other things for his mind to dwell on, of course, his own well-being following the arrests foremost among them. But now that he had apparently escaped any reckoning there, maybe his murder would visit upon his conscience. It should, he reasoned, the administrator was no more guilty of misdeed than he, and yet he felt nothing for the man, no matter how he tried.

His worry about being followed would not leave him, though, and he began to take more care as a result, after so many days spent living at the point of the sword, sticking to neighborhoods he knew and places where he was certain other Nohritai would be. He doubted it would make any difference if someone really meant him ill. He had seen men assassinated in drinkeries and beaten senseless on the streets with no one present bothering to lift a hand in aid. It was the way of existence in Darrhyn, and it would be no different for him. It did not occur to him to stay off the streets, to avoid the drinkeries and public rooms, he supposed, because part of him wanted to find out who was behind this discomfiting sensation. He no longer cared about the cost.

Each morning, Masiph went for a morning chew at one of his favorite public rooms in Isinan, known only as Jahrel's Corner, after the Nohritai who, decades ago, had chosen the place to conduct all his business. It had been a drinkery or an academy then, depending on who one talked to, and in the intervening years it had changed hands many times and been named many different things by its owners—the Arms of Gethuil and the Cock's Crow among others. Those who attended the place in its various guises, as well as all who passed by, ignored those names, persisting in calling it Jahrel's Corner, long after the man had joined his ancestors on the higher plain, and long after any knowledge of who he had been or what family he had been a part of had slipped away.

Jahrel's was one of Masiph's favorite public rooms simply for the name. He loved the idea that a man's name could live on through the years, absent any knowledge of his achievements or family. It was a comforting thought, for obvious reasons. He always sat at the same table—inside, not on the street, with a clear view of the door. He passed in and out of an animated conversation taking place among those gathered around him about the tomb defilers, who had not only continued their desecrations, but had even begun stealing the bodies from the mausoleums. The discussion concerned what they might be doing with the sacred remains. Ransoms were suggested, as well as dark alkemya of some sort.

There was a tap on his shoulder while he listened, which froze him for an instant. Masiph turned around, hoping to see a familiar face, but instead it was a stranger, almost as nervous as himself. A small man, not many years older than himself, he stood a tentative distance from where Masiph sat, his hands working together in a reflexive, almost unconscious gesture. Masiph saw that he was sweating and his eyes were dead from some elixir he had taken. Seeing that, along with the man's clothes, he relaxed. Probably he just wanted some coins to buy a chew, though in his state he wouldn't be able to taste, let alone feel its subtle effects.

"You Masiph, Husem," the man muttered, his teeth clenching around the words.

Masiph went still and finally nodded.

It seemed to take a moment for the man to register it. "Someone out back. Wants a word."

"I don't think so."

"No," the man said urgently. "No. Needs a word."

Masiph smiled, preparing to dismiss him and return to the conversation, conscious that some at the table had begun to watch what was happening. The man appeared to struggle with a thought and then spoke over Masiph.

"About the Luessan," he said, clearly pleased that he had managed to recall this bit of information.

The whole table was watching now, and Masiph stood with a shrug and a shake of his head, as though he had no idea what the man was referring to. He clapped his arm around the man and started for the entrance, ignoring his protestations that Masiph needed to go to the alley. Once they were out front, Masiph pushed him away with a smile as if to send him on his way.

"No, no," the man said, turning back to him and pointing to the public house.

Masiph punched him in the mouth, sending him toppling to the ground, his legs and arms going every which way. It was much harder than he had intended, and he felt bone and tooth give way at the force of his knuckles. The man rolled to his knees, blood welling from his mouth, which he probed with a finger, as though it were not his own face that had been struck but someone else's. He looked up at Masiph, helpless and confused.

Masiph kicked him with the side of his boot, not hard, though it knocked him to the ground again. "Get out of here, cur," he said. "Get."

The man scrambled away frantically, moving so quickly that he stumbled over his own feet and fell headfirst with a cry. He got up again, looking to see if Masiph was following him, and then ran into the crowded street without looking where he was going.

Masiph watched him disappear into the passing crowd before glancing back at the Jahrel's, but no one there had followed him out. He looked around and saw only the regular passersby on the street. None of them met his eye, either fearful of or oblivious to what he had just done. His hand began to ache and he clenched and unclenched it, wondering if he had broken a bone. *Ancestorforsaken fool,* he thought as he looked at it. He had broken the skin on one knuckle, but other than that it seemed fine.

His initial thought was to flee, though he hoped in a slightly more dignified fashion than his messenger just had. But something stayed him. He reached into his robes to confirm that his dagger was there and started around the street to the alley's entrance. This was utter madness. Whoever was waiting for him, whoever had been following him, had to be one of his fellow conspirators. Nazeed, maybe, since Masiph had seen no evidence that he had been taken, or perhaps someone Osiphan had hired looking to silence him, or exact revenge for whatever wrongs he was presumed to have committed. Maybe they thought he was the one who had betrayed them. Nothing good could come of going to see.

He stepped cautiously into the alley, staying as close to the wall and shadow as he could. If they had a bow or darts he would already be dead, he decided, and so, after a moment's pause, he stepped away from the wall and moved farther down the alley to where the public house was. There was no one there that he could see, though the alley turned with the street up ahead. He looked above to see if he could get a view of the surrounding roofs. The building opposite the chewing house was a brothel, laundry lines strung from all the windows on its upper stories across the narrow alley obscuring what lay above.

Sensing someone behind him, he swore aloud, in spite of himself, and when he turned she was there facing him.

"I hear you've been looking for me," she said, her voice a threat and an invitation. He nodded. She looked at his hand and he realized that he had drawn his dagger. He put it back in his robe, flushing. She walked past him, her eyes flashing and the hint of a smile touching her full lips. He followed her into the streets, neither of them uttering a word.

Lisser had said she was both the vulture and the carrion. Those words echoed in Masiph's mind now that he was face to face with her again. She would not talk of herself at all, though Masiph had many questions. There was, in fact, very little in the way of conversation after she found him. Her silence worried him—well, everything about this worried him, but, he told himself, he would not be here if she did not desire it, whatever her reasons.

A series of scars ran parallel down her back between her shoulder blades, disappearing behind the flowered robe she wore, the type any courtesan or common trull would wear beneath her outerwear when receiving a man. Each cut made to form the scars had been deep and had healed to a ridged whiteness. Some of the tribes found in the north marked themselves in this manner, he had heard. He longed to run a finger along one, tracing it from her neck down to where it disappeared and beyond. He asked her where she had gotten them from. It seemed a better question than from whom.

She looked him over coolly from where she stood, seeming not to blink. The robe was sheer and opaque simultaneously, so that he could see the shadows of her nipples, and yet the closer he studied them, the less apparent they were. He felt like a fumbling idiot here, a boy with his first woman, awaiting that moment when he would be initiated into her ultimate mysteries. She poured them both cups of wine and handed one to him, making sure their fingers touched in the exchange, before sitting in the chair across from him, crossing one long leg over the other. That this was the exact pose she had struck when he first glimpsed did not escape Masiph's notice.

They were in what he assumed were the quarters where she received her clients. It had the appearance of a courtesan's rooms: a long couch for reclining, wine and cups at the ready, a lyre for music, and a large and well-appointed bed. From where he sat, near a table that had playing cards and die set upon it, the bed was just within the periphery of his vision, never the focus with her just across from him. She was, Masiph noted, just beyond his reach. He wondered if these were in fact her quarters, for there was something generic about the whole room. A courtesan of standing had rooms with her own personal touch throughout, not to mention gifts from lovers, both past and present, prominently displayed. This room felt more like something an academy bawd would put together for those clients who fancied themselves worthy of a courtesan, but had not the coin for it.

She sipped her wine and he, as if he had been waiting for a signal from her, gulped hungrily at his, though it made speech no easier for him. She studied him from over her cup and he felt himself getting aroused, and his face went flush. He was certain she noticed both. There was something predatory in her gaze, the cold indifference of a panther, without judgment or feeling.

"Has your tongue gone sodden?" she said, breaking the silence and startling him. He opened his mouth and swallowed, words failing him again. Here was all he had longed for these last mad weeks and all he could think of now as he stared at those lips was the Luessan merchant who had met his unfortunate end at her hands.

"You've rambled and rambled looking for me and now you've no appetite. Or are your stones paving other roads?"

"No," he said. "No, I've the appetite for a banquet and supper both. And the talent for it."

"That remains to be seen." She looked away from him, touching her finger to her lips.

"Are these your rooms?" he asked.

"I am my own gentleman usher and counsel-keeper."

He cleared his throat. "Then why am I here?"

"I am sorry," she said, an easy smile breaking across her face. "You thought you would be the bird building in this nest. Have you not heard that I am the cat of the mountain?"

"I was told you were both vulture and carrion."

"More the vulture. More the vulture."

He nodded, unsure where this was going.

"And what of you? Are your badge and seal more than mere baubles that might strike a poor maid's fancy?"

"You will have to see that for yourself," he said.

"Well then," she said, and rose to her feet, setting her cup on the table. Masiph did so as well and, after a moment's hesitation, he embraced her, placing his lips upon her supple ones. He tried to capture every sensation, seizing it and holding it in his mind as though it were the most precious of treasures. Her scent, that same elixir of wildflower from their first encounter, the taste of her lips, the feel of her hands upon his back, and her breasts pressing against his chest—all of it threatened to overwhelm his reason.

After what seemed a delicious eternity, she released his mouth from hers, her lips wandering along his jaw and up to his ear as though she were about to whisper her utmost desires to him. He felt her tongue upon his earlobe and exhaled, closing his eyes. Her tongue disappeared, though, and before he realized what was happening she had bitten his ear—no playful nip, but enough to draw blood. He gasped and tried to jerk his head away, but she still had a hold of him in her teeth, her hands strong on his wrists.

When at last she released him and stepped away to look at his now-pale face, there was blood on her scarlet lips. He thought of the Luessan merchant as he watched her lick them clean. Gen frog poison, Lisser had said she used. Masiph was not sure, but he thought the poison only needed to touch the skin to work. He tried to think whether the merchant had had any marks on him, but could not remember. She was smiling at his confusion and panic, and, in spite of his immediate fear, he was even more deeply aroused.

"I know your badge, Masiph den Ibrazol," she said. "And the Ad Ezern seal."

He did not remember leaving, where he wandered after, or what, if anything, he had said following her revelation. She had not said anything further, he was certain, but why would she? She had already said it all. His fate was now in her hands. It was not clear to him what would happen next. She would ask for coin, of course, to buy her silence, and he would have to find a way to provide it.

What evidence did she have that he had been there at the Luessan merchant's home? Or did she even need any? She had her own word and the state of the Luessan to prove her own presence at the scene, and then it would just be a matter of convincing Ibrazol that she had seen Masiph there. A difficult task, but one he felt certain she was capable of. There was nothing he could do. He still did not know her name and, he felt certain, if he returned to the quarters she had brought him to she would no longer be there.

By the time he arrived home at the Ad Ezern estate, Masiph's hands were shaking and his sight was blurred. Had she drugged him after all, he wondered in a panic? It took all his effort to reach his quarters, and once there he collapsed upon his bed and drifted into oblivion.

# 34

"It will do you no good to say nothing. You will talk eventually. Everyone does."

Tehh said this in a friendly, conciliatory way, a comforting smile on his face. Both were at odds with his words, and, Hieran saw, his eyes, which never left those of their prisoner. They were in a cell behind the Qraul's corner, installed after one of many bloody melees in the halls during Council, for the Qraul's men to dispense a quick justice on those who disturbed the peace. Tehh sat on the chair one of the Kedaui Guard had brought for him, while the attendant sprawled on the floor where they had chained him, studying the toes of his boots. Hieran moved restlessly along the wall between the two, glancing from face to face, until a glare from Tehh froze him.

"Now," the Adept said, "let us begin again. Why did the Golden Veil kill Fedyl Kugisyr?"

The attendant said nothing, his eyes staying on his boots, his fingers worrying at the chains on his wrist.

"What does the Veil have planned for today?"

No response, though Hieran thought he detected a hint of a smile tugging at the prisoner's lips. That told him all he needed to know.

"How many of you are there?" Tehh said, as though he were a lady of rank needing to tell the cook how many fowl to prepare for the celebration.

Hieran ground his teeth in frustration. It was like watching a youth seduce a maiden at a festival dance. They had no time for this; whatever the Veil had planned was going to happen during the speeches. Though all involved certainly enjoyed the songs that came from their lips, they could not be expected to occupy the better part of a day in talking, which was what would be required if Tehh kept up this manner of questioning.

As if sensing his impatience, Tehh changed his tact. "I have given you a chance to see reason and cooperate. That time is at an end."

He paused to give the attendant an opportunity to speak, and shook his head sadly when the prisoner maintained his silence.

"Then we shall scour you," he said, and stood looking at Hieran to see that he was ready.

The High Adept had begun to work his way toward his conclusion, a stirring one no doubt, but Keleprai had no ears for it. On the table beside him were strewn notes from the various Gvers, along with his reply to Byuvir, which the Disciple had failed to deliver. Now both he and Tehh had disappeared, ostensibly because of a Golden Veil plot, and he was left only with his attendants. One did not trust servants to deliver notes of any sensitivity, he knew, unless you could be certain they were illiterate.

The risk for him now with what he sought to do—turning the Gvers against this war without losing his standing with the Qraul or the High Adept—was simply too great to leave in any but the most-trusted hands. Tehh would know that better than any, and his absence now, at the very crux of the moment, spoke volumes. The only people he could trust with the task were Kigarle and his man—Donier was his name, nobles of rank both, standing watch at the corridor entrance. But if the Veil were truly preparing an attack of some sort upon the Council, it might not be wise to send one of his guard away. It might be just the thing he was expected to do in this situation, leaving him vulnerable to whatever plot was in motion.

Byuvir and Duirhe were watching him, probably the others as well, their faces betraying nothing, but they had to be wondering why he had not responded. They would have seen him receiving other notes from his attendants, reading them even, and doing nothing in turn, his hand never stirring his quill. What is he about, they would be thinking, and Keleprai had to wonder himself.

As Cepedutherupt began to speak of the alliance he had forged with the Renians, not mentioning the price paid in coin and vows, Keleprai rose from his chair and retreated into the corridor. Let them wonder at that. He conferred with the senior attendant there.

"No, Most Gracious," the man said, "there has been no attendant from the Adept. Would you like me to send one to him?"

He waved the man away. It would do no good sending attendants out; he had no idea where the Adept was. Why had the old fool not sent anyone? He was not so bereft of his senses yet. It told its own story, of a piece with the entire day's proceedings. And when it came down to it, Keleprai had no trust for Tehh, and no matter what the High Adept might say, he believed the old man had been involved in some way with the attack this spring. Too much was still unexplained.

And now he wanted Keleprai to betray the High Adept—to what end? No matter that he agreed, that it made sense; there was always something else with that man, some other game being played. *The Golden Veil.* They had not been heard from in five years and here they emerged, today of all days. It did not pass. It did not.

The High Adept began his final flourish by setting his face sternly. "Have no doubt, the Shadows, now more than ever, constitute one of the great evils in this realm. They are a blasphemy against all that our Council and the proper use of alkemya represent. Many gathered here dismiss evil in this profane realm; they say it is mere rhetoric that things are neither wholly one nor the other, all aspects intermingled. Ten years ago that was shown to be wrong, and it seems in the time since we have forgotten the price paid there for our inattention.

"There is evil in all realms; it breeds if left unchecked, taking root in the field like any common weed. But the Gods offered us balance in all things, so though there is evil in this existence we are offered the chance to oppose it, to bring a balance to creation. Let us not forsake them or our duty."

With that, his speech was ended and Keleprai joined the other Gvers in their rote applause, landing his fist on the table cluttered with unanswered notes. His irresolution suddenly galled him. Here they were on the precipice of a war, and regardless of his doubts about it and Tehh and the High Adept, he needed for once to act. The Realm would not come to him. It never had, he realized now. It slipped away, further and further from his grasp with each moment.

No more. He turned to take up his quill.

The low hum of chatter from the passing crowd seemed both to grow louder and to accelerate, as though a wave were passing through the various courtiers and hangers-on, cresting somewhere beyond where Donier and Kigarle stood at watch. It did not help to settle Donier's already-frayed nerves, for it was clear now that something was happening further up the corridor, and judging from the many veiled glances cast in the direction of Keleprai's box it involved the Adept and Disciple of Lastl.

None of it surprised Donier; he had been expecting this from the moment the Council session had begun, and now the time was upon him. He tried to remember what Uherl had told him in the drinkery that morning. It would be a simple thing, a message carried, or a moment's inattention. When would the request come and from whom? He cast a sidelong glance at Kigarle, who was also peering nervously at the growing excitement of the crowd. The latter, at least, was obvious.

As several members of the Kedaui Guard hurried through the crowd, causing everyone to stop and crane their heads, the excitement growing more palpable by the moment, one of the Gver's attendants stuck his head out from the corridor. "The Gver wishes to speak to you," he said to Kigarle, who glanced significantly at Donier, or so it seemed to him, and followed the attendant up the narrow corridor, where the Gver stood waiting out of sight of the Council chambers. Donier watched them confer for a moment before remembering himself and turning to face the corridor, which seemed to grow louder with whispers by the moment. There were any number of men who idled in the recesses created by the half-columns, some of whom, Donier was certain, had been there for some time, their eyes flicking from those passing by to the various entrances to the Gvers' boxes, including the one he stood watch at.

He felt exposed as he stood alone, and his head began to ache from the tension he felt building in the room, everyone certain that something was happening. Various scenarios began to play out in his mind, each ending with him standing over the bloodied corpse of the Gver, that besotted fool, surrounded by the accusing glares of the gathered crowd. As these thoughts crowded his mind, a man in anonymous robes materialized at his side, touching his arm briefly, his eyes scanning the crowd.

"Don't stare at me," the man said under his breath. His voice was so quiet Donier could barely make out what he was saying, and he had to resist turning to stare at his lips. Instead he looked at him from the corner of his eyes, studying his face and clothes. He was unremarkable to look upon, a placid and uninteresting face, the sort that would gain someone entry anywhere with the robes to match. A man of rank clearly, but what rank Donier could not hazard a guess. His accent placed him from Craitol, but to Donier that meant little. He did not need to be told that this was the moment Uherl had told him would come. Sweat began to trickle down his back.

"When Kigarle returns, you must make yourself absent," the man said.

"How am I to achieve such a thing now? They know the Veil is about. There will be questions," Donier said, his words sounding high and fast. He tried to swallow.

"A reason will present itself, I am sure," the man said in reply, putting an edge of command to his voice. He was gone, disappearing into the crowd before Donier could think of a reply.

He looked around to see if anyone else was watching and had seen the brief conference that had occurred. No one seemed to be looking at him, even among those who idled nearby. Still, Donier could not quiet the anxiety that seemed to grow even as the volume of the talk around him built. The Veil agent had brought with him more questions than answers, for if Kigarle were involved in some way with their plot—and Donier had no doubt that he was—why not have him find a reason to allow Donier to be absent? Unless he had been wrong and Kigarle was not with the Veil. That did not stand to reason, though.

When Kigarle returned from his discussion with the Gver, he looked, to Donier's eyes, more at ease than he had since their arrival in Craitol. It was as though whatever burden he had been carrying these last days had been lifted from his shoulders, its weight no longer pressing against his soul. Panic seized Donier for a moment as he wondered if the attack had already taken place, but when he glanced down the corridor he could see the attendant pouring wine into a cup for the Gver.

Kigarle passed him a handful of notes, marked with the Gver's seal, unable to disguise his satisfaction. "The Gver has asked that you deliver these and return any responses."

Hieran did not know whether his head hurt from the screams or the alkemya, but it was throbbing in rhythm with his pulse. Agony was always present when he became Tehh's engine, no matter how small the task, forming the germ of alkemy and having it ripped from his being for the Adept to use. And, as always, once the Adept had seized his being, prying at it for the seed he needed to sprout, the world went black, his vision disappearing. The smell of the transmutation occurring was heavy in his nostrils, a rotting decay, a gangrenous limb split open.

The rattling of the chains that bound the attendant told him the man was still conscious, writhing on the floor.

"Tell me what the Veil has planned," Tehh said, allowing the attendant a brief respite from the scouring.

"You cannot do this. It is against Council law."

"All laws have exceptions," Tehh said, and began again.

This, Hieran knew, was not precisely the case. It was forbidden, without exception, by Council law, but the authority of the Council, even amongst its own Adepts, was no longer seen as the final arbiter in such matters. Not after what had followed the end of the northern war, when Council Adepts hunted for those of Kercubegahedd's agents who had survived the battle and scoured them to ruinous husks or worse. One of Tehh's enemies on the Council might try to have them both censured for what was occurring here, if they were to somehow find out, but they were unlikely to succeed. Tehh was too important, and they were on the High Adept's ground here—he would undoubtedly approve of their actions.

"What are your plans?" Tehh said through the attendant's screams, relenting with the scouring only when he fell silent.

Hieran breathed a sigh of relief, the veil lifting from his eyes. He steadied himself against the wall, letting his stomach settle as well. Intermingled with the smell of transmutation was the stink of feces and urine, the attendant's bowels having released when he lost consciousness. He looked an absolute wreck as well, his face pale and lined as though he had the fevers. Hieran winced as his senses drew it all in, but Tehh appeared unaffected by the sights or smells of the room. He sat down on the chair and waited.

The attendant shuddered awake with a gasp and began sobbing. "No more, no more."

"You know what you must do."

"No. No."

They began again, Tehh not even rising from his chair. The man screamed and begged, an endless babble of words, most of them half formed.

"What is happening today?"

"Nothing, nothing, I swear it. I swear it. Nothing."

"Why kill Fesyl, then?"

"It was only him. He had been talking about us. About everything. I was told to take care of him during the Council. That's all."

"Don't think you can lie to me," Tehh said. Both Hieran and the attendant shuddered as the Adept began to work the alkemy again.

"No more. Mercy," the attendant said. "I will tell you everything."

"See that you do."

The attendant raised himself up so that he could look Tehh in the eyes. "I do not know what is planned—please! Let me finish. I was not told. It was true what I said about Fesyl. He needed to be killed. The reason to do it here was to provide distraction from what else the Veil has planned."

Tehh considered this for a moment. "You do not know why they wished to cause a distraction? And why involve the other man? Who was he?"

"I don't know who he was. I was never told."

"I don't believe you."

"No. Please don't," the man cried out as Tehh raised a hand. Hieran was relieved when the Adept did nothing, nodding for the attendant to continue.

"They did not want to attack Fesyl until he met your Disciple. They knew he would. The other man did not know your man's face, so they asked me to signal when the two met and the other man was to make sure that your man knew the Veil was behind the attack. Upon the Gods, that is all I know."

"Upon the Gods?"

"Upon the Gods, upon my soul, upon my very life."

"That," Tehh said, rising to his feet, "is already forfeit."

He turned and left the cell, Hieran on his heels, leaving the attendant to his sobbing.

# 35

They had still agreed to nothing, promised nothing, but at the very least they had not yet decided to kill him and be done with it, Vyissan thought as he made his way back to the Vazeir's Palace and his rooms. Yet. It was small consolation, but he clung to it. He might not be able to convince them to go along with the High Adept's designs, but he could still hope to somehow engineer his own survival. If all had gone well today, which he thought it had, he might have achieved that much already.

He and the Vazeir were returning to his palace through the baffling series of tunnels that lay beneath the whole courtyard, connecting the various Imperial Palaces. Who knew where else they led? Presumably some provided an avenue of escape from the city. He found it all completely fascinating. There was nothing of its like in the Realm. Was it possible that these corridors extended throughout the entirety of the capital?

The Vazeir led the way, holding up a lantern as a guide. The limited circle of light cast by the flame only added to the impression he had of these works extending to realms beyond realms. In addition to the winding corridors that branched off one another like vines climbing a wall, there were rooms that would emerge out of the tunnels, without warning, from which there would be a number of possible exits and, in some cases, stairways leading up or down. The entire effect was such that he had no sense of where he was in relation to the ground above. He could imagine a vast warren unfolding deep into the bowels of the earth, where souls might be lost on their way to or from Ulternon's Hall.

The maze suggested nothing of the kind to the Vazeir, Vyissan thought as he peered at the man's always inscrutable face through the glare of the lantern. He was not sure what the Renians or the Enir believed in terms of an underworld. The plains that they believed in could not be crossed by the living, only by the dead, and, even then, only under the rarest of circumstances. One was condemned or blessed to a particular plain depending on one's actions while in this realm. Their ancestors were involved, after a fashion, as well, though Vyissan was unsure of the specifics. Even if their creed allowed for such speculation, Vyissan was certain the Vazeir would not be the one to engage in it.

There was much debate among the various sects of Craitol as to whether Ulternon's Hall, which housed the dead, could be reached by the living. There were stories of those who had, but they were obviously myths. Vyissan felt that, as the Hall was somewhere beneath the earth, it stood to reason that it would be possible to reach its doors, though why one would want to he could not imagine. It was interesting to think about. He had read the fine work by Danir, a poet of the north, about a man's journey to the Hall through a series of halls and mines, inhabited by dwarves, demons, and those spirits who had been exiled from the Hall itself. A work of fancy, which some had called blasphemous. He had found it a pleasant diversion, even if it did indulge in some of the more outrageous superstitions of the common folk.

The Vazeir was not one for pleasant diversions. He had taken the lead in questioning Vyissan in both his audiences with the Ad Eselte, the Emperor preferring to observe, his expression one of kindly thoughtfulness. The audience began, as had the last, with an apology for his detainment in the Vazeir's Palace, which, he was sadly informed, must continue due to circumstances in the capital. Vyissan offered no protest to this, though he knew that, regardless of the circumstances in the capital, they would not want the emissary of the Qraul wandering about at will.

He was first asked to go over the agreement he had proposed at their last audience, three days before, but that was not the point of this audience. What they desired was proof that he was what he claimed, an Adept, for that was the crux of everything.

That was a simple trick, for what did they know of Adepts and Disciples and alkemya? He gave them a court show, the sort of feats any half-rate village conjurer with the rudiments of Council training could perform. The audience chamber the Ad Eselte received them in had the benefit of several windows, giving it ample light. Vyissan used that to do what Adepts and their Disciples often referred to as Charlatan Feats, simple tricks using the alkemy drawn and shaped from the astral within the room to bend the light, creating illusions.

There was some art to it, though most on the Council disdained it, and some were better than others, and Vyissan was certainly one of those. He showed the Emperor and the Vazeir a representation of Craitol and the Palace of the Qraul, following that with images of his journey up the river from Sylaron, making sure to include the burned ruins of the town struck by the Shadow Men, concluding with an image of Darrhyn as he remembered seeing it at sunset that first night with the blue domes of the palaces just in view. The images were all obviously just that—no better than the sorts of landscapes one could buy on the streets from calligraphers in any town—but impressive nonetheless, since they appeared to materialize from nothing.

Both men were careful not to betray their reactions to his displays. "An impressive feat, no doubt," Vazeir said. "You have learned much of our realm."

Vyissan felt himself go cold, though the sun was still warm on his back. This, after all, was the realm where all the writings of the Art had been burned, along with many Adepts. It was a treacherous line he was forced to walk, and he could not know when he would spill off it.

"Yes, Husem," he said. "I have never seen the like of it."

"Indeed. And this"—a wave of his hand where the images had appeared—"this is related to the communication you have with your compatriot."

"After a manner, yes, Husem. We have yoked ourselves together as two ardeh plowing a field. If we pull in unison, images may pass between our minds."

Here the Vazeir was unable to disguise his true feelings, revulsion showing plainly on his face. He glanced at the Ad Eselte, as though he were unsure of how to continue.

"And this," the Emperor said, a frown on his face as though he were considering some philosophical problem, "is possible at such a distance."

"Not without difficulty, Most Gracious. But yes."

The Ad Eselte shook his head. "A marvel. But at what cost, I wonder?"

Vyissan nodded, unsure of what to say.

"I know nothing of these abominations that you practice on yourselves," the Ad Eselte continued, "and it is not for me to say whether an Enir should or should not be committing such acts. Your ancestors will decide that when the time comes. Something else troubles me about this proposal of your Qraul's, for the cost is dear to him as well. And I wonder why he is willing to spend his coin so freely in aid to a rival."

"The Qraul fears the Shadow Men may grow so powerful that no one will be able to oppose them, Most Gracious. And as for the silk, it is my belief—and my Qraul's—that it is always better to make friends than enemies on this plain, for our time is so short."

It was nonsense, all of it, and likely both knew as much. Not that it mattered; the silk and the coin it represented to the Empire had been calculated to carry the weight in this discussion. He would just have to wait and see if it would.

They had left it at that, nothing decided and no indication of when or what the decision would be. The Vazeir had not said a word to him as they passed through the tunnels, as always keeping his counsel to himself. When the two of them emerged from below into a spartan room, different from the one they had used to enter the labyrinth earlier, the Vazeir extinguished the lantern and curtly bid him good day, leaving him to wait for his escort. Not a man for fancy, that one, Vyissan thought. He was not left alone long as the taciturn guard, whose name Vyissan still did not know, arrived to lead him back to his quarters.

As they passed down one of the main corridors of the palace, which Vyissan assumed connected the Vazeir's rooms to his wife's, a Ceinobyte approached. The courtiers he had encountered before on his meager taste of the world beyond his cloistered realm had paid no mind to him, an Enir under guard apparently unworthy of note. The Ceinobyte, by his expression as he neared, wanted to speak with them.

He smiled and placed his palms together in genuflection before them. "Seliccen, the days are kind to you?"

The guard seemed perturbed, but he halted. "They are, Ahednar, thank you. And yours, I would hope."

"As well. Thank you for asking." The Ceinobyte paused. "I have not seen you at the sanctuary in some time."

"I was away from Darrhyn for a time and I've been busy since I returned."

"Of course. Remember that you are always welcome. As are you," he said to Vyissan, who thanked him.

"Ancestors grace you," Ahednar said, and blessed them both, touching his left hand to each of their foreheads before going on his way down the hall.

Vyissan and the guard continued on, turning down the corridor that led to his quarters. There was something odd, Vyissan thought, about the Ceinobyte being in the Vazeir's Palace, though he couldn't say why. Perhaps it was just that the Vazeir seemed a man too practical and of the world to care that much about religious contemplation. He was unlikely to deny others that opportunity, Vyissan supposed. He turned to ask the guard about it in time to see him collapse to the floor.

He looked down at the man, struggling to comprehend what was occurring. There was a loud humming in his ears and simultaneously the feeling that his hearing was dimming. He had to get to Hasen, to let him know. He was immediately confused as to where he was and where he needed to go. He tried to call out, but his tongue was dry and his jaw refused to move. As he took a step forward, his vision swam with sudden color, blurring the corridor into a swirl of light that soon disappeared into an ever-expanding darkness, and he felt his legs go beneath him.

# 36

Donier stared at the notes in his hand, running his finger along one of the seals. How fragile they seemed, how immaterial. His mouth worked, trying to form words that would not come forth.

"Nes Donier," Kigarle said, interrupting his thoughts, "you must go. Time is of the essence. The Gver will be speaking and he must have answers before he does."

Donier swallowed, fear paralyzing him further. What had the agent said to him? A reason would present itself and here was Kigarle furnishing him with one. Could he leave the Gver alone, unguarded in effect, with a man he knew to be in the Veil? Did he have any choice in the matter?

He mustered some words. "Should I not...is it wise to leave only one of us on watch with the Veil about?"

"The Gver is aware of our position," Kigarle said, unable to disguise his happiness. "The notes are of such grave importance that he is willing to chance what may come."

Donier nodded. "Of course. I understand. I am always at his service."

He gave an awkward bow to Kigarle, wondering why he was doing so as he did it, and headed into the teeming corridor, exhaling loudly, his eyes stinging with tears, knowing he had just condemned the Gver to death. His emotion surprised him given that he despised the whore-rotted fool, but fool or not, he did not need his death on his conscience. As he walked down the corridor, shoving his way past people, holding the notes up above the crowd, he tried to find some excuse that would return him to the Gver's box. Somehow he had imagined that events would conspire to thwart the Veil's desire, sparing the Gver, and he would escape blameless in the eyes of all. The Gods were not so kind, it seemed.

As he made his way around the Qraul's corner, the Disciple emerged from the crowd, one of the Kedaui Guard at his side. His visage was shocking to witness. It looked as though he had spent a week going without rest or sustenance, sleeping in his own filth, and yet Donier had seen him less than an hour before, looking well. He did not need to ask what the transformation had been from. The Adept had been busy then. When the Disciple spied him through the crowd, he grasped Donier by the arm, his bloodshot eyes widening in disbelief.

"What are you doing?" the Disciple said.

"The Gver sent me to deliver these," Donier said, holding the notes up.

"No," the Disciple said. "We have to return now. His life is at stake."

A hush of anticipation followed the Herald's announcement of Gver Pervelte's name to the assembled. He rose to his feet and bowed in the direction of the Qraul's throne, a faint smile on his lips. An infuriating smile, Alieren thought, and she was glad again their meeting had been conducted in darkness so that she had not been forced to look upon that. She would not have been able to control her anger. Even still, and though she hated herself for it, she allowed a measure of hope to steal into her being that somehow Pervelte would have changed his mind.

"I have thought long on the matter of the engines, as long as any in this room. And I have sacrificed more than any as well," he said, raising the stump that remained of his left arm. "So when I speak, I speak with the authority of experience and, I hope, wisdom."

He paused to consider each of the Gvers, one by one, and the silence in the room deepened as everyone waited to hear what he would say.

"I cannot countenance such actions as the High Adept proposes. I believe it to be folly to face the Shadow Men on the ground of their choosing, for they shift as the dust does in the air. But the High Adept has my utmost respect; he has considered these matters as well and he knows the fate of the Realm may turn on them, one way or the other. And he is apparently willing to shoulder those consequences. For that I say, while I do oppose this war, I will not stand against it."

It seemed to her that the Gver was looking at her as he spoke the last fateful phrase. She also noted, as no doubt everyone in the chamber had, that he had not once acknowledged the Qraul in his speech. He made plain his intent: let these fools have their adventure in the desert and I will bide my time. Just as he had said to her. Dark days indeed.

Byuvir a Kylep was the next to speak. He seemed to grow fatter every year—they all did, these men, their evenings spent in feasting and wine and their days in ceremony. He shared a glance with Gver Keleprai and she wondered what the meaning in that could be. The Alastl looked awful, his shade pale, his eyes bloodshot and heavy. It was as though he had aged years since his arrival, though what might be troubling his blood she could not fathom. Everything had gone to plan for he and the High Adept.

"Most Illustrious Qraul, Most Radiant Qraulla," Byuvir began, bowing to them both. "These are heavy times, as the High Adept has made plain. And as my ally from Pysel has said, the ground can shift easily, in the desert especially. This cloth must be measured carefully. What is best for the Realm? A border free of Shadow Men incursions, no doubt, but is such a feat achievable? Realms free of the blasphemy of the engines, but how are we to ever stop those who wish to craft them?

"Have no doubt, these questions weigh upon us all, just as they did ten years ago. We all remember the price paid then? We all paid it, some more than others." And here he nodded at the Qraul and Pervelte.

"Can we countenance such a price again? The High Adept speaks of evil taking root if we do not. I fear the bloom of youth shall wither and leave only rot in our limbs. It is a grave, grave risk our Qraul asks us to take, and we should not be blind to it in our considerations."

Byuvir paused and wet his lips with a cup of wine, looking about the room from box to box, his gaze coming at last to rest upon the dais where the thrones rested. The attempt to heighten the moment felt false to Alieren, the other Gvers seeming to pay no mind to his theatrics. Keleprai, she noted, had risen from his seat and retreated from sight, no doubt preparing for his own speech.

"I stand with our Qraul," Byuvir said in a momentous tone. "The chance to strike a real blow against the Shadows cannot be passed on. By the time it comes again, we may be like the Renians and looking at the shards of our empire."

Duirhe was next, talking for some time on much the same theme as Byuvir, but Alieren had stopped listening. All these empty words. All ceremony, form demanding that something be said, though the decision had been arrived at long before this, only the price to be determined. Though she was forced to sit here in silence, her efforts mocked or ignored, she would choose not to hear. She glanced at Laterala, his face, as always, attentive. Beneath it she could sense the brimming excitement that must be peaking now that Pervelte had abdicated and the rest of his Gvers had fallen in line. He would have his war, the bloom of youth sold for some coin.

When Duirhe was through, he sat down and the Herald announced that Keleprai, Gver of Lastl, would speak. His chair remained empty and he did not appear at the announcement of his name. A ripple of sound went through the room, low with consternation, everyone craning their heads to peer within the Gver's box to see what was going on.

Donier fought his way through the swirling crowd, back the way he had just come, sweat pooling on his back beneath his robes. He was aware of the furious glare of the Disciple upon his back as he went. The insufferable whoreson, not even of rank, had chided Donier for his dereliction of duty and handed the Gver's notes off to the first of Qraul's attendants that the guard with him could summon, not even bothering to give the man any instruction before starting toward the Gver's box. Though he dearly wanted to heap scorn about the Disciple for the abuse he was suffering at his hands, Donier knew better. The man was right, after all—the Gver was in danger.

It all occured right before them in an instant as they struggled against the swelling mob, every individual seeming to move at cross-purposes with them. Kigarle ducked his head into the corridor, an attendant or the Gver himself calling to him. At that moment a man detached himself from the stream of passersby and moved toward Kigarle, being careful to stay out of his line of sight. He was a peninsular by his shade and wore the robes of the Qraul's attendants, but Donier knew he was nothing of the sort. He gave a shout, calling Kigarle's name above the din of the corridor.

Kigarle turned at his shout, panic on his face as he looked wildly about the corridor for Donier. By the time his eyes settled upon the peninsular, it was too late and the man was upon him, slashing a dagger across his face and chest in two quick blows before sending him tumbling to the ground. The assassin stepped over the stunned and bleeding Kigarle, disappearing within the Gver's box. Cries of horror erupted from those nearest the Lastl box, causing everyone to stop in their tracks, craning their heads to get a glimpse of what had happened.

Donier ran, a man possessed, throwing people aside as he went, ignoring their cries of outrage. He drew his sword as he came to the entrance to the Gver's box and saw the assassin, his blade raised above his head ready to plunge into Keleprai's eye. It was like a scene upon a tapestry, everyone frozen in the moment, poised to act but never allowed to do so. He could see the Gver frantic, mouth agape as he stared a the dagger's point, fumbling with his robes for his own weapon. Behind him an aghast attendant stood, clutching a bottle of wine, the blood drained from his face.

That was the scene for an instant, as Donier crossed the threshold of the box, sword ready to strike, a moment forever where fates could be decided irrevocably. It dissolved as he continued forward, the attendant falling to the floor in terror, while Keleprai gave up trying to find his dagger and stepped back, raising his hands up in a feeble attempt to ward off his attackers blow. Only the peninsular remained as he was, poised to strike, but somehow unable to. Donier could just see his face in profile, his mouth contorted into a grimace of triumph, the awareness that something had gone horribly wrong beginning to slip into his eyes.

Donier did not stop to wonder just what was staying the assassin's hand. He moved with a sure purpose, raising his sword and bringing the blade down heavy upon the man's neck, taking most of his head off in the process. The peninsular stayed frozen as he was, even as his head flopped over to rest on his shoulder, blood erupting in geysers from his neck. He remained like that for so long that Donier, thinking he could not be of this realm to survive such a blow, raised up his bloody sword again, determined to finish the job for good, when whatever force had held him was released and his body toppled to the floor, a small sigh escaping the lips of the already dead man.

As the pool of blood spread about their feet, Keleprai gradually lowered his arms, color returning to his face, and he said to Donier, "Eternal thanks. You have saved my life."

Donier nodded, his eyes not leaving the corpse. All he could think was that in saving the Gver's life, he had forfeited his own.

Hieran, exhausted and still trying to regain his equilibrium after scouring the attendant and thwarting the assassin's attack against the Gver, struggled to recall the name of the Qraul's Master of Offices who had summoned them to another of the chambers beyond the Qraul's corner. He paced back and forth in front of them, leaving the Disciple lightheaded just trying to follow his perambulations. The Master—Eilhaun was his name—was a slight man who had retained some of the look of a youth, though he was far into his days now, and he seemed one of those fastidious courtiers whose obsession over the endless details of court and its ceremonies assured his rise through various offices to this pinnacle. A thoroughly dislikable man, in other words.

"Why was I not informed that you had a prisoner involved in the incident?"

"That is a question for your men. They caught and held him," Tehh said. He looked tired, Hieran thought, the efforts of the day taking their toll on the old man. The Disciple could only imagine how he looked given how he felt.

"And your duty to the Qraul and the High Adept?"

The Master of Offices had been furious when he discovered that an assassination, and another attempted upon a Gver, had taken place without his being informed. It did not speak well to the Kedaui Guard or his organization of the day, but these things always happened at Council it seemed. He would not see it that way, Hieran knew. And the fact that Tehh had not bothered to send to Eilhaun word of what was occurring...he would naturally see as a sign of betrayal. This was his domain, after all, and all served him within these walls, excepting the Qraul and the High Adept.

What did it matter, anyway, Hieran thought in annoyance? The day and the deeds were done. The High Adept had his war and the

Gver had survived. Investigations would be conducted and reprisals would take place, the Veil responding with their own, and so the cycle would begin again.

Tehh, Hieran was glad to see, had little time for the fastidious Master. "That I saw to when I dealt with the prisoner and the assassin. Did you see to yours?"

Eilhaun snorted. "Is there danger of more attacks today?"

"You have eyes, as well as I. The Council is done. Decisions made. The crowd is gone." Tehh shrugged. "They will try again, certainly, but not here."

Eilhaun pursed his lips in thought. "And is Adept Weirn involved in any way with this, do you think? His man was in the Veil, after all."

"And killed for it. But the Council will have to investigate." Hieran nearly laughed. There would be a thorough investigation, Tehh would see to that, and any link that could be found between the Adept and the Golden Veil, no matter how tenuous, would be proffered to the Council so that Weirn could be sanctioned. And on it would go between them.

Eilhaun stopped his pacing in front of the Adept, leaning forward to meet his eyes. "Are they rising again?"

"Who is to say?" Tehh said after a moment. "The man who was murdered told my Disciple that he had been involved in the attack against Gver Keleprai and the High Adept. If that was in fact the case, and we will have to revisit our investigation to find out for certain, then we will have to rethink a great many things."

"There was an engine used in that attack?"

"Indeed there was."

"A diversion. perhaps?"

"A hopeful thought," Tehh said with a laugh.

Eilhaun frowned. "What are you suggesting?"

Tehh stood and shook his head, the taste of a smile crossing his lips. "Whether we go to the desert or stay here, the engines will persist. Those we deny power and who desire it will turn to them always."

The Master of Offices shook his head. "So you always say. They are blasphemous. The Gods shall ensure our triumph."

"Perhaps, perhaps. I fear that it is like a drip of water on a rock. For all our strength, given time, and time is their greatest asset, they will wear us away."

Elihaun's frown deepened and it seemed he was intent on continuing the discussion, but Tehh had already started for the door, shuffling his steps. Hieran followed behind, his own legs unsteady, and together they returned to the Council halls.

# GLOSSARY OF TERMS

Abapolly: mythical demon from Kragi

Ad Eselte: title of emperor in Renuih

Adept: practioner of alkemya

Aesen: canal in Darrhyn

Alkemy: the latent power within all elements that can be released by transmutation

Alkemya: the practice and study

Anchonites: monastic priest in Renuih

Ardeh: animal, raised for its wool, milk and meat

Asieren: Ad Ezern paradise in Renuih

Aslyn: leaf that is chewed

Astral: aspect of elements that contains alkemy

Asyl: psychotropic nectar

Ceinobyte: Renian priest

Celes: Ad Reteln paradise in Renuih

Cohort: Craitolian amy unit

Corenedor: Renian officer in the army or Watch

Craitol: Realm of, as well as capital of the Realm; westernmost realm in all the lands

Cureders: Craitolian priest

Dala: beans, drink brewed from

Darrhyn: imperial city of Renuih

Devew:city and river in Kragi

Disciple: practitioner of alkemya, Adept's subordinate

Dravasyl: drinkery in Darrhyn

Elen: city in Renuih

Enir: a distinct religious sect of the Renian people

Enir Republics: once part of Renuih; now independent city states along the coast between Renuih and Craitol, south of the desert; inhabited by those of the Enir sect

Eresnan: River between Darrhyn and Sylaron in Renuih

Esyln: jewel of the Renian Empire in the desert; now a ruins inhabited by the Shadow Men

Fegh: city in Kragi Province

Gver: Craitolian lord, governor of a particular territory

Haigah: mountain city on the border between Kragi and Craitol; a mountain pass

The Hashil: central boulevard in Lastl

Hasierren: Lasisen sanctuary in Craitol

Hessen: Enir Republic

Hesite: district in Takyl

Hezier: ruler in the Enir Republics

Hjai: second to a Vazeir in Renian Imperial administration.

Hueithel: neighborhood in Darrhyn

Isinan: a street in Darrhyn

Kastril: Renian fruit

Kenir: coin of Renuih

Kragi: province in the north of Craitol; once an independent realm

Kulez: northern city in Renuih

Kylep: city in Craitol; seat of a Gver Byuvir

Lasisen: a sect of worshipers of Senteur in Craitol

Lastl: city in Craitol; seat of a Gver Keleprai

Lethle: city in Kragi Province

Luessan: one of the three eastern kingdoms that broke away from the Renuih Empire

Luisel: town in Renuih

Magister: officer of law in Craitol

Magisterium: building of the Magistery

Magistery: officers, or the office itself

Melinon: Craitolian goddess of the earth

Mgetir: island south of Craitol

Morning, Midday, Evening: factions in Craitol

Mythres: powder made from flowers native to Kragi

Nrai: port city in Craitol; one of the contestants in the Sea Challenge; seat of Gver Assuard

Nohritai: nobility in Renuih

Nuerrallah: one of the great sages of Reniuh

Qraul: ruler of Craitol

Quadra: unit of the armed forces in Renuih

Quicksilver: an element capable of inhabiting all constitutions simultaneously and decaying the astral of any substance

Pyrsedies: forts guarding the desert frontier in Craitol

Psyel: city in Craitol; seat of Gver Pervelte

Rakai: port city in Craitol; involved in Sea Challenge

Renuih: Empire in the east, former rulers of the desert

Sanader: religious authority in Craitol; usually has authority over a particular city or region

Senteur: Craitolian god of the heavens

Shadow Men: the people of the desert; also referred to as Shadows or by other pejoratives (demons, beasts, etc.)

Suliher: honorific for those in the Renian Watch or Army

Sylaron: major port city in Renuih

Takyl: city in Craitol; seat of Gver Duirhe

Tolote: coyote-like animal of the desert

Tson: city in Craitol; seat of Gver Hythel

Tuissar: Enir Republic

Uenam: district in Darrhyn

Ulternon: Craitolian god of the dead

Usgelt: city in Kragi Province

Vazeir: imperial administrator in Renuih

Watch: protectors of the imperial city Darrhyn

Xln: port city in Craitol, involved in Sea Challenge

Yuehilth: prison in Darrhyn

Yseltez: city in Craitol; seat of Gver Issilar

# ABOUT THE AUTHOR

Clint Westgard is the author of The Shadow Men Trilogy and the science fiction epic The Sojourner Cycle, the first volume of which, The Forgotten, was published in 2015. In addition, he has published a work of historical fantasy set in colonial Peru, *The Maleficio Chronicles*, and a retelling of the Minotaur legend, *The Trials of the Minotaur*. Clint Westgard lives in Calgary, Alberta.

# ALSO BY CLINT WESTGARD

*Dance of Shadows*
*Volume Three of The Shadow Men*

War with the Shadow Men looms in both realms as the consequences of the Gvers' Council in Craitol begin to make themselves known. A war that could end in glorious triumph or bitter disaster.

Doubt shadows everyone's steps, for they know there are no certainties in the desert. Especially now the Shadow Men have made the art of alkemya their own.

No one has more questions than Vyissan, for he is working in service to a cause he is no longer sure he believes in. And now he must undertake a journey with those who both loathe and fear him. Before the first sword is drawn, his life will be under threat.

But his will not be the only one, for somewhere in the desert the Shadow Men lie in wait…

# ALSO BY CLINT WESTGARD

*The Forgotten*
*Volume One of The Sojourners Cycle*

Who is David Aeida? And what does he know that has so many
people pursuing him?

David doesn't know. He can't remember anything about who he is.
But he finds himself ensnared in a vicious conflict between a
religious cult and a guild that patrols the crossings between
multiple universes. They will both stop at nothing to gain whatever
knowledge he possesses. Most dangerous of all, is the implacable
hunter, known only as the Seeker, who has his own reasons for
wanting to find David.

His only hope is to recover his memories before they do. His only
ally is a woman named Meredith, and she definitely knows more
than she is telling...

Spanning both universes and the human mind, *The Forgotten* is an
unforgettable science fiction thriller that questions the very nature
of identity. It is the first volume of the *Sojourners Cycle*, an epic that
will encompass the fates of universes and humanity itself.

# ALSO BY CLINT WESTGARD

*The Maleficio Chronicles*

Luisa is always more than she appears. Rumor and mystery surround her. And strange events seem to follow wherever she goes.

Born in Lima, City of Kings, to a noble family, her father so fears her true nature that he banishes her to a convent. There she falls under the suspicion of the Inquisition and decides to flee.

Disguised as a man, she embarks upon a series of wild adventures, dueling, carousing, and gambling her way across colonial Peru. But everything changes when someone recognizes her for what she truly is, and soon she finds herself fighting for her very survival.

In a world where she will always stand apart, Luisa undergoes a strange journey, marked by betrayal and murder, terrible powers and mysterious strangers. *The Maleficio Chronicles* is her incredible confession and a story like no other.

# ALSO BY CLINT WESTGARD

*The Trials of the Minotaur*

In the fifth year of the rule of Auten the One Eyed a minotaur is born to one of Colosi's most important families.

Taken from his mother as a newborn, exiled and cast from his family, the minotaur vows to return to the imperial city and take his rightful place as a patrician in the empire. But the patriarch of the family, his grandfather, will stop at nothing to see this blemish to his honor destroyed.

And so begins an epic journey, through lands beyond imagining, marked by despair and exile, triumph and betrayal. At its heart lies a quest to be free.

www.ingramcontent.com/pod-product-compliance
Lightning Source LLC
Chambersburg PA
CBHW051251250626
47155CB00009B/3255